MW00773777

THE RISING

This book has been published with
financial assistance from the
Arts Council of Great Britain

THE RISING

A Novel by
EDGAR WHITE
(Nkosi)

Marion Boyars
New York · London

Published in Great Britain and the United States
in 1988 by Marion Boyars Publishers
24 Lacy Road, London SW15 1NL
26 East 33rd Street, New York, NY 10016

Distributed in the United States by
Kampmann & Co. New York

Distributed in Canada by
Book Center Inc, Montreal

Distributed in Australia by
Wild & Woolley Pty Ltd, Glebe, NSW

British Library Cataloguing in Publication Data

White, Edgar
   The rising: a novel. — (The pygmies and
   the pyramid; bk. 1).
   I. Title   II. Series
   813[F]   PR9265.9.W/

Library of Congress Cataloging in Publication Data

White, Edgar, 1947—
   The rising: a novel/Edgar White.
     p. cm.
   I. Title.
   PR9275.M653W4837   1988
   813—dc 19   87–36839

ISBN 0-7145-2878-1 Cloth

Typeset in 11/13pt Baskerville by
Ann Buchan (Typesetters), Middlesex
Printed and bound in Great Britain by
Biddles Ltd, Guildford and King's Lynn

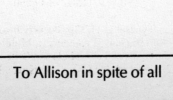

To Allison in spite of all

Se levantan los ninõs

The Bird in the Young Girl's Thighs

Let's start here: the eyes of the child looking. From the beginning he was strong and then he grew stronger. They called him Legion and hoped that would be the end of it, but it wasn't.

He and his friend Solo walked the long hot road toward the rum-and-grocery shop which Mr Shields owned. Shields' shop was the centre of all village activity. Solo had persuaded Legion to come with him.

'You going see something today.'

He had taken a chance going with Solo to Shields' shop. He knew if his mother heard he had skipped school it would be certain 'licks'. Eyes watched them as they approached. Some hushed greetings passed. The other boys were used to playing truant. They were regulars, but Legion felt terror in his heart and his skin already anticipated the beating.

Tall-boy was already there.

He was a youth in his teens. The warrior whom everyone followed.

Legion and Solo were small but they hoped someday to be
Tall-boy because Tall-boy knew no fear. He had already
spent time in HMP, the prison with the large gate which the
boys would sometimes pass in front of and whisper.

Tall-boy was always graceful and would never bend. If
something fell he would retrieve it with his bare foot.

Tall-boy glided over to the counter where Mr Shields was.

'Mr Shields, sir, you all right?'

'Fine, Tall-boy.'

'Nice, nice. You could let me hold one of them cokes, you
know.'

Mr Shields gave an upward glance as much to heaven as
to the Coca-Cola sign above the bar.

'You have money?'

'Rest you self no man. Me say I want a coke.'

'Me ask you if you have money.'

Tall-boy sucked his teeth in disdain and, making a
backward glance at his gallery of supporters, said to no one
in particular:

'Is which one of you barefoot boy going pay this man for
me? I don't want to have for kill him. I kill two man already
and I tired.'

The boys just laughed. No one volunteered the money.

'Solo?'

Solo looked up, a bit surprised at hearing his name called.

'Yes, Tall-boy?'

'Let me hold few shekel, and check you Friday.'

It was not a request but a command. Solo didn't want to
pay but he was glad for the attention. The others looked at
him with respect. He emptied his pocket and then
commanded Legion to do the same.

Legion had the greater amount because he had two pockets in his trousers whereas Solo had only one without holes.

The money was rendered up.

'Right,' said Tall-boy.

Mr Shields took out the bottle of coke.

Tall-boy touched it with two fingers and then, looking away, said: 'Give me a next one, this one not cold.'

Mr Shields' face tightened, but he didn't want trouble with this boy. The last time they clashed his store was mysteriously robbed that very night. The police were tired of dealing with Tall-boy; he had worn them out and led them to conclude that he must have ice for blood. He seemed to welcome pain. Now they decided to wait for an offence which would put him away forever.

Mr Shields brought out another bottle of coke from the ice box. This one Tall-boy accepted. He always drank coke because it was the most expensive soft drink on the island. He liked it because the Yankee boys drank it.

He held the bottle aloft and drank majestically, and when he had all but drained the bottle he suddenly passed it to Solo, like a chalice, and walked off.

The other boys whispered together: 'Style!'

Solo took one swallow and let Legion have the remaining one, then they followed after Tall-boy. Outside, the sun shone at its noonday zenith. Even the trees were sweating now. Tall-boy sat on a rock beside the road. No one dare join him.

Soon a girl came past carrying a small bundle. She moved casual and easy. As much because of the sun as the fact that she didn't want to appear to be seeking anyone in particular.

But eyes caught her. Eyes travelled along the long slim legs and the smoothness of skin below the orange skirt.

When she passed Tall-boy she gave a small nod of her head but acted as though she hadn't really meant to see him. The orange head-tie matched her skirt. When Tall-boy spoke to her she placed the bundle atop her head and held her arms akimbo at her waist as though daring him.

'Watch this now,' said Solo to Legion.

They observed the ritual from across the road. Tall-boy and the girl exchanged defiance for a while and then they crossed over to Shields' shop. The girl took out some money from a small black purse. She sat down for a time before Tall-boy ordered a Guinness for himself and a coke for the girl.

Mr Shields wanted to pass a remark but decided better.

Tall-boy put some coins in the jukebox and changed the nothingness of the shop to a cool glade.

Some time passed and all eyes studied as Tall-boy carefully touched the girl's long legs without ever once looking at her directly. The other boys pretended they didn't see. Only Legion kept staring. Solo chided him.

'Don't watch so hard, he going get vex.'

When the drinks were finished, Tall-boy ordered two crushed ice cones and then casually walked out with her.

Soon after, Solo told Legion to come on. They followed them, keeping well back. After a time they saw Tall-boy lead the girl off the road and along a pathway leading to the beach.

'Is what they go do?' asked Legion.

'What you think man. They go do pussy.'

Legion tried to act casual but he knew Solo saw his ignorance. He had never seen people do it although he heard sounds coming from a house once. The architecture of the houses made it common knowledge to anyone in the islands, but Legion's mother had never had any man come to their house.

They hurried after them and in his haste Legion stepped on a lizard. The feel of it underfoot was more terrifying than seeing it.

Solo started to laugh, but kept on so as not to lose sight of Tall-boy and the girl. He soon spotted them because of the bright skirt.

'Ssh, don't make no noise.'

They watched in wonder as Tall-boy started to lie down in the girl's lap and she gave him a small packet from inside her bosom. He rolled a large cone-shaped spliff and smoked. Thick clouds of smoke went up to the sky.

Legion wanted to ask Solo about it but he felt foolish.

Solo had seen everything because he never went to school. Whereas Legion had to give an account of all his time, Solo had no one to give an account to. He lived between houses and families, so they called him Solo.

Tall-boy finished smoking and as he took one last full breath of smoke he made the girl lean over him and suck it from deep inside him into herself. She did not like to smoke but she didn't mind taking it like this.

They kissed slowly for a long time and then she was no longer over him but beneath him.

She told him to be careful of her skirt. So they moved over to the grass. She spread a large shawl down and he came over her.

The skirt was an island skirt, short and easy to lift. Her panties slid off in one motion.

From the angle Legion was looking from he could see a

small bird take off from the ground and climb into the air. He blinked his eyes twice to make certain. It appeared to him as if the bird came from between her thighs.

Tall-boy moved inside her downward and she came up to take him.

Legion could see her hands working on his back, making small patterns, and then he heard her calling out although he couldn't tell what she was saying. It sounded like 'God, oh God.'

Legion wondered why she was saying that. He saw her long legs entwining but there was too much that he couldn't see. He turned to Solo, who was smoking and trying to keep from laughing out loud.

He had to get closer and see the act itself. Legion pushed the branches of the tree which were hiding them from view. The girl heard the rustle. She stopped and looked up. She saw the boys and started to scream.

Tall-boy jumped up and picked up two stones, which he pitched at them with deadly accuracy.

'Go way, you too damn fast. I bet you me lick out you damn eye for you.'

Solo took off and Legion was at his heels; still, a stone caught his back. He cried out but didn't slacken his pace until they were back along the main road.

'You see what you do, you get us catch. Is chupid you chupid.'

Legion felt foolish: he should have been more careful but he had to get a better look.

They parted ways. Solo was going to collect Wilson's goats — he made money from doing odd jobs like that.

Legion, meanwhile, had to go home and look as if he'd

spent the day at school. He wouldn't go with Solo because Mother Francis could always smell the goats on his clothes when he came in.

The two boys looked at each other.

'Catch up,' said Solo.

Legion was glad, for this parting gesture meant he was forgiven.

'Yeah, catch up,' he answered, and went off. His shoulder still ached but it had been a good day. Another ritual. And he liked that word. That warm and close-liquid word. Pussy. He said it over several times in his mind and then entered the fear of his house.

Legion walked slowly along the path towards his house. He did not want to be early on his supposed return from school. He stopped by the large hollow tree trunk where he'd hidden his school book and pencils, checked to see that he wasn't observed, then gathered them up. When he entered his yard he walked first around the back garden where the water hose was and carefully washed all traces of dirt and bushes from his feet. He dried himself and then entered the house as quietly as he could. He saw his mother in the kitchen preparing dinner. She looked up and noticed him. It was as if she felt his presence before she actually saw him.

'You home, Rudie?'

She always called him Rudie, which was his first name, but he preferred Legion.

'Yes, Mumma.'

'You was good in school?'

'Yes, Mumma. Is Mother Frances awake?'

'Go see, no. She asked for you.'

He went quickly upstairs to see Mother Frances. Everyone called her that. He always went to see her first when he came home. They got on well.

He entered the room and called out: 'Mother Frances.'

'You come?'

'I come, yes.'

The old woman was in bed. She adjusted her head tie to make certain that her balding head was well covered. The small candle which she burned night and day was flickering. She had taken to burning it over the last five months because she'd not been well. The old people always burned candles and incense to keep death away when they saw it coming.

'You feel all right?'

He could see her eyes flickering like the candles.

'Is what you bring for me?'

'I don't bring nothing today you know.'

She laughed. 'You mean you didn't bring a sweetie for me?'

'Not today, Mother Frances.'

She smiled wickedly. 'Well then, I not going dance at you wedding.'

Sometimes he would bring candy for her from the market on the way home from school, but today he had not gone that way and besides he had no money left since he had to give it to Tall-boy.

She patted the bed. 'Come sit by me, Legion.'

He came over and sat on the bed. She didn't allow anyone else but him to sit on her bed.

She opened a box which had some cookies that a neighbour had brought for her.

'To show you I'm not bad-minded you could have some of
cookies.'

The cookies tasted of ginger.

'Tell me about the time when the volcano blow up,
Mother Frances.'

He had heard the story many times before, but it still held
a fascination for him. The Soufriere volcano on the island
had never erupted in his time.

'Well, it was a time like so . . . I was still small like you.'

'I not small.'

'All right then, you not small, I was big like you.'

'What things was like then?'

'Like now, boy, some had much and some had nothing.
Some people eating 'til them belly swell and others just
eating dust.'

In his mind he tried to imagine people hungry enough to
eat dust.

'In them time so, if a man catch you nyam a mango from
off his tree he chase you with a machete. Well, one day we
hear this rumbling like thunder you know. But when we look
up to the sky we no see no rain at all at all. So now we wonder
what this.

'The first noise come and then it's quiet quiet. Then after a
time it start again and we see this blazing light from top the
mountain. A next explosion.

'Everybody start to run. The chickens and goat start to
bawl and people saying that the world coming to an end. Me
mother take we inside. . .'

'You was fraid?'

'I was fraid, yes. All of we hide under the bed and hold
each other tight and me mother start to pray for God to spare

us. Outside was full of grey mist so thick you couldn't see. And the smell, oh God, it so bad you couldn't breathe. It was the sulphur from inside the volcano.

'A lot of people get burn from the hot ash and houses catch fire. I hope you never see it. . . It come like devils loose out of hell.'

He was lost inside of her story, imagining the flames and the darkness and chewing down hard on the ginger cookies, when he happened to glance from the window expecting perhaps to see the Soufriere volcano erupt. What he saw, though, was not the volcano but something far worse. He saw Teacher Biddy enter the path leading to the front of the house. She stopped to admire some flowers in the garden.

Legion's heart started to race. He knew that truly now was the end of the world. At first he thought of running down the stairs and maybe stopping her, telling her that his mother was ill, but already it was too late: he heard their voices downstairs.

Could he perhaps slip outside the back door? But where could he go to hide? He would have to come home some time.

He just sat frozen, no longer hearing the tale his grandmother was telling.

'Something wrong, boy?'

'Oh no, nothing.'

Then he heard his name being called from downstairs. He did not like it when his mother called him in that tone.

'Rudie! Rudie!'

'Yes, Mother?'

'Come down here boy.'

He excused himself and went downstairs slowly. Very slowly.

'Yes, Mother?'

'Hear him, "yes Mother". You don't see Teacher Biddy here, you not going to say hello to her?'

'Hello, Teacher Biddy.'

The old woman gave him a mocking stare and tilted her head questioningly.

'Teacher said she can't see you today, she want to know if you sick.'

The boy didn't answer; he looked down at the floor.

'Well, is sick you sick? Answer no, what happen something wrong?'

'No.'

'No what?'

'No, Mother.'

The fact that the teacher was present made his obligation to be respectful double. The teacher folded her arms in her lap as she sat.

'Come here, Rudie.'

He walked over to her.

'You know that it's not good to play truant from school, don't you?'

'Yes, Teacher.'

'I expect to see you first thing tomorrow.'

'Yes, Teacher.'

The teacher rose and brushed her dress with her hand. She turned to the mother.

'Well, Mistress Barzey, spare the rod and spoil the child.'

'I know, Teacher, I go deal with him, don't you worry. He must have been with those young scamps he love to follow so much. But they go do for him, them nasty boy them. Thank you for stopping by, Teacher.'

Legion started to walk back upstairs as they stood in the doorway and exchanged whispers, but no sooner had he reached the third step than he heard the door shut and the hurried footsteps of his mother.

'Where the strap? So you is a man now. You learn how for lie and hide already.'

The leather belt caught him about the legs. He tried to jump but it was too late. He got two good licks in before he could reach the sanctuary of Mother France's room.

'What he do, Desmie?' she asked.

'Teacher say he never go to school this morning, and someone tell she them see him at Shields' shop.'

'All right, all right, he won't do it again, will you boy?'

'No, Mother Frances.'

'He won't do it again, Desmie.'

'You don't see you spoiling the boy. He already going on like he some little prince. He come in cool cool like he ain't do nothing. You too brazen, boy.'

She gave him two more quick ones with the strap which he tried to ward off with his hand.

'That's enough, Desmie, you see, he crying.'

'You just let me catch you again. You need a man's hand to straighten you out. Go you room.'

She held the strap threateningly and he raced out as a light flick caught him on his bottom.

He heard them talking.

'It's not the boy's fault he don't have a father.'

'Oh Mother, please don't start.'

'Is you freeness which bring him into this world.'

He closed the door and lay down on his bed. It was not too bad. He knew he was lucky. Yet he could expect another beating tomorrow at school. Teacher Biddy would cut down a tamarind switch from the bush by the school house. She was an expert with the switch and knew how to cause maximum pain. She was never put off by tears — she had been teaching for twenty years and had beaten both him and his mother. He knew what that 'see you first thing tomorrow' really meant.

His mother made him wait for his supper. Then he was sent straight to bed. He did not sleep for a long time, images raced through his brain. He weighed everything up and decided that it was worth the double beatings for the day's experience. As sleep took him he thought again of the young girl and Tall-boy, the thing they did together in the grass.

He dreamt of her. And the tiny bird he was certain he saw fly up from between her thighs.

Sunday: day of rest in the islands. Dawn comes on too early and catches the still entwined bodies of lovers, making them flee before the sudden return of husbands. Women sing hymns at almost six a.m. behind their fences of corrugated iron.

Some wash clothes early so as not to be discovered working on the sabbath day. Animals are lazy, knowing little will be expected of them on this day. At seven, services are broadcast from Radio Paradise and are received over battered radios.

The old women dress in white or black, arm themselves with bible and hymnal and advance on various churches. Some stay behind to cook and attend later eleven o'clock services, secure in the knowledge that lunch will be there waiting on return. Sunday, day of rest, prayer and gossip.

But today was Easter Sunday and Legion rose early. Not because he wanted to but because hands removed him from the liquid warmth of sleep. His mother made him bathe and dress for church. Not that she wanted to either, but Mother Frances would not hear of missing service. She had decided it was time to make an appearance back in the secular world. Rumour was fast about that she was dying or dead. It had been five months since she had gone abroad. She had thought to wait until this Easter Sunday; it would be a fitting time for a re-birth.

Legion was made to wear his new brown shoes which hurt his feet. His discomfort didn't matter. What mattered was that the shoes came from the mysterious country across the waters called America. The place of all good things.

He must be seen to wear them because the other island boys at best could only wear second-hand shoes which were passed from brother to brother, or maybe father. Most had no shoes at all.

His mother dressed in one of her good number of dresses. She was never in the same dress twice in public in the same year. These too came from America.

She dressed carefully, enjoying the silk of the underwear and the nylon of her stockings. The thought that some girls on the island had one pair of panties made hers feel all the nicer.

When they were ready the car was brought around to the front of the house by the driver who was summoned. He was not really a chauffeur but functioned as one whenever he was needed. This he didn't mind doing. Not only was he well paid but he also had access to the car, since neither Legion's mother nor Mother Frances could drive. There were in fact two cars, not for ostentation, but because usually only one worked at a time. The driver's name was Perkins. He was tall and had a secretive face. Legion had never liked him.

'Perkins, come help Mother down the steps, please.'

'Yes, certainly.'

He put out a cigarette and took leisurely steps towards the house. He gave Legion's mother, Desmie, a long look which she ignored, but Legion noticed. He then went indoors and helped the elderly woman down the steps.

Once outside, Mother Frances paused to take note of the garden. She checked to make certain that each flower was in grace. She gave instructions to Perkins, who also saw to the garden and the repairs to the house. He pretended concern and then opened the gate, then the door to the car. The old woman entered first, then Desmie and then Legion, who paused to check that his flies were in order and his tie tied.

The slow descent into the town then followed. Perkins wanted to speed but he was checked by Mother Frances.

'Perkins!'

'Yes, Mother Frances?'

'You feel you in a race or what?'

'No, Mother Frances, I'm not racing.'

'If you go so fast I can't enjoy the ride. Beside, I want people to see me.'

'Yes, M'am.'

And so every few feet the car stopped to accept the greetings of the concerned friends who had not seen her for so long.

'And how are you, Mother Frances?'

'So long I not seeing you.'

'But look, it's Mother Frances, how well you look. I was just asking after you yesterday self.'

And to all the old woman answered: 'Praise God.'

Once in the church she received the immediate nod of the minister, Preacher Parks, who now felt a special need to preach a strong sermon. The church was well filled, being Easter. There were a large number of flowers on the altar and a full choir. The congregation all knew their respective seats in the pews. The wealthy were placed in prominent seats and the poorest closest to the back, where they could enter late and leave early. The girls on one side of the church and the boys on the other, where they could see each other and not do much harm.

The windows had been opened well in advance since it would be a hot day and Preacher was threatening a memorable sermon.

As soon as the service started, Legion began to feel hungry.

Half the congregation was staring at Mother Frances, the other half at Desmie and her new clothes.

The hymn was called and soon dark choruses of 'O God Our Help in Ages Past' were heard. Some old men kept the bass part steady. Some women violated the treble.

There followed a word of thanksgiving for the appearance of Mother Frances, to which the older women echoed: 'Praise be to God.'

Then followed several testimonies of how God personally entered several lives. Two women repented of their former lives and three men told of the misery of drink and sin before they met with God.

Then Preacher attacked his sermon about Christ being left alone to pray and his two disciples who fell asleep and could not keep the watch.

'Could you not watch with me even one hour?'

When the congregation was sufficiently beaten into guilt, the collection was taken.

It was felt that Preacher deserved it. He was bathed in sweat, his fat round face glistening like a polished mirror.

And then there was the announcement of the week's activities in the parish. Everyone was weary and hot by now, and little more was expected until suddenly Miss Greenaway rose to sing. Miss Greenaway was a strange woman, solitary and thin, but she had a presence and somewhere inside her a powerful voice.

She sang 'Were You There When They Crucified My Lord?' Every note came clear, moved from inside her and into the bodies of everyone who heard.

Outside in the street, passers-by came pushing their faces against the windows. Tears came from Miss Greenaway's eyes but few could see them because they too were bathed in tears.

Then it ended as suddenly as it had begun. It moved from remembrance to memory. And there was a stillness in the church which even Preacher Parks, in his ignorance, was frightened to disturb.

After the service, tea and cakes were served downstairs to aid the building fund.

Legion loved the final parting hymn. To his mind it meant the coming of freedom. The release.

Everyone milled about the various benches they used for pews. There was no great hurry to depart for now was the time for the quick gossip.

'I see Mrs Jenkins no come today. I guess she too weary from last night. I see the Ice Man enter she yard late and me never see him go out.'

'For true?'

'So it really be sister.'

'You hear Janice make a baby.'

'Is who the father?'

'. . .eh eh, but she not shame how she could be worthless so?'

Preacher Parks stood solid by the door of the church secure in the knowledge that his sermon was a good one. There was much rivalry among the preachers of the district. When Mother Frances passed he gave her his most penitent and profound expression. He paused only momentarily to glance at Desmie.

'We've all been praying for your speedy recovery, Mother Frances.'

'Why thank you, Preacher.'

'You've always been in our minds. Each week I ask for you. But you're looking much improved.'

'Praise God, I feel little better now.'

He then turned to Desmie and held her hand a moment too long.

'And how are you, Desmie?'

'Fine, thank you, Preacher.'

'We miss you at choir practice.'

'Well, I've been busy caring for Mother.'

'Well, I certainly hope we'll be seeing more of you.'

She withdrew her hand. Preacher Parks was aware of it. He knew certainly that he was not in her class and had little chance of access, but where there was life there was hope, after all.

Had he perhaps been with another church, the Church of England, with its possibility of social mobility, he might have been able to work his way from village to town and then, possibly, abroad. Such was not the case with the Pentecostal Church. It was not like the Catholic Church, a vast chess board of offices and coups leading to bishoprics and riches. The best he could hope to do was represent his district at a convention. If he had the gift of self-hypnosis, which the best preachers had, there might have been a chance; but he was at best a plodder. He could dominate country girls into repentance and seduction, but not anyone like Mother Frances' Desmie who had two cars and a house larger than his church. So Preacher Parks settled for tea instead and refused the offer of rum raisin cake, and waited.

Downstairs, Legion chased around with the other boys and kept a vigilant eye on the girls' toilet, hoping to catch a quick view of something dark and uncovered. Failing that, he drank lemonade and listened to the old women announcing the catalogue of the more recent deaths in the parish. And so it went in a circle: birth, sickness, death and food.

Then the car suddenly reappeared with Perkins, who had a scent of rum and lime on his breath and a mischievous smile on his face.

Soon they made the ascent back up the winding hills to the large white-painted house.

Mother Frances stopped once more in the garden, smelled the oleander and then retreated inside, assisted by Perkins.

Carol was one of three housegirls who spun around the Barzey household. She did the washing and cleaning, ran

errands and assisted the dressing and undressing of young
Legion Rudie Barzey. Carol was Legion's favourite
housegirl because she would do nice things for him in the
dark. Sometimes she gave his whistle a pull when she washed
him. And at special times let him suck her breast. For as long
as he could remember she had been doing this and making
small whimpering noises in his ear. It was because she had
seen his mother breastfeed him when he was a baby, a thing
she did briefly for she soon tired of it. Because Carol was
jealous of the fact that she had no milk, she tried to imitate
the action.

Carol had long thin legs but nice size breasts and a
rhythmic way of walking that gave promise that she
possessed a body beneath her clothes despite her thin frame.

The relationship had been a good one. Carol did not seem
to mind fetching and carrying, she could certainly use the
money (which her mother never failed to take), as well as the
free food. Outwardly it did not seem to bother her that she
was the same complexion as Desmie Barzey and yet,
whereas she had only one change of underwear, Desmie had
more than she could remember, often changing three times a
day. Carol accepted this Karma and merely helped herself to
what she wanted. Others called it theft. She called it need.

Desmie had been to boarding school where she learned
how to sit with her legs closed and hold a cup and saucer. She
learned French, piano, needlepoint and penmanship. The
fact that she never learned to boil water never alarmed
anyone. The world was filled with Carols and Daisys and
Mabels who could.

Carol had big feet which couldn't endure more than an
hour in a shoe. Her mother would tell her: 'You is just a big

foot neaga girl from bush. You eye them too damn wide. Mind you don't make baby fore you time.'

From age twelve she was a full woman and daily she would test Legion to see his growth.

'It not long enough yet, Legion.'

'When it will be long enough?'

'I tell you when, don't worry.'

'What you go do then?'

'Give you something nice.'

Until then he had to content himself with fingering her, and getting what instruction he could from Solo, who learned from Tall-boy.

Mother Frances never trusted Carol. She had a way of looking at the girl which would make the fifteen year-old squirm.

'Tell me, Carol, you haven't seen a dollar which was on the table here last night, have you?'

'No, Mistress Frances, me no see nothing.'

'Yes, I thought not. Tell me, Carol, you could read?'

'I can read and write me name, M'am.'

'I see. Tell me, you know what the HMP is?'

'Yes M'am, is jail.'

'You know they does hold *woman* and man in there?'

'Yes, M'am.'

'Good, Carol, very good.'

Carol's favourite activity was sitting by the side of the road with her skirt hitched up and staring dreamily at the men driving by in cars. Her ambition was to own a radio and eventually a record player like the one Desmie had. She tried to get the boys she dealt with to buy her these things, but the most she ever got was a dress.

One Monday Legion hurried home quickly after school. He was eager to see her. He would not chance playing hookey again from school; the prospect of another double beating was a little too much for him. He had been thinking about her all day. He had seen her in church that Sunday, in her white dress, and her skin looked bright, as if she had bathed. In school he could not keep his mind on sums and Teacher Biddy caught him daydreaming. He knew what he wanted to do with her. He wanted to spend a whole day with her, experimenting and trying to make a bird fly from between her thighs. He would have to make do with a few hours behind the house though. He hoped she would be there when he reached home. He raced through the bush, taking a short-cut home. He scratched his arm on the branches of trees but he didn't care. When he reached home he saw her bending over, dusting the table. He looked to see where his mother was. She had gone out with Mother Frances and Perkins. His heart was still racing from the run.

He crept up behind her and stuck his hand up her dress.

She spun round and slapped him.

'You too damn fresh, little boy. Go way. I bet you I set fire to you tail.'

She struck him again several times and reached for the broomstick. She swung viciously at him, catching him once across the face. He had never seen her like this. He looked down and saw drops of blood on his shirt.

Still she kept screaming: 'That's all you want, all you men too damn wicked.'

He called out: 'Carol, stop.'

'I go kill you, I go kill all of you.'

He couldn't understand why she had suddenly changed like that. He had done the same thing to her many times and she had laughed. The most she would do was push his hand away or sometimes pretend she didn't feel it and close her thighs tight with his hand between. Now she was mad, her eyes wide with hatred.

Then suddenly she caught herself. She noticed the blood running from his nose.

'Oh Jesus, what I do? Oh God, Legion, I sorry.'

She ran to get water and a cloth. She started wiping his face.

Legion didn't cry. He wanted to but the desire to hurt her was greater than the pain.

'I go tell Mother Frances.'

'No, don't tell. I sorry. You want me give you something nice?'

'I go tell Mother and she not go let you come back here.'

'Don't tell. You not like that. You know me and you is friend.'

'Why you lick me then?'

'I don't know. Is not you, is somebody trouble me.'

'Who, a man?'

'I can't tell you.'

She started to clean the bloodstains from the floor. The nose had finally stopped bleeding.

'You not go say nothing to them, right?'

'You go give me what I want?'

'What you want?'

'Take off all your clothes.'

'Suppose they catch me naked here?'

'We could hear them when they reach.'

He took her upstairs. She took off her dress which came over her head easily.

He looked at her. She was like he saw her in his mind in

school. He made her take off her panties. She laughed at him as she took them off.

He looked at her in wonder. He had never known there was so much hair there. She told him to suck her nipples. He obeyed.

'Oh God, not so hard boy.'

He started to rub the hair between her legs. She was laughing now but he started to feel dizzy, something was happening to him. She pulled him down on top of her warmness and he called her name.

'Carol.'

She took him in her hand and the dizziness came on more. Then they heard a car coming. He didn't want to believe that it was really a car.

She jumped up: 'Oh Jesus, look me cross.'

In two seconds she had her dress back on and was running and stepping into her panties at the same time. By the time they entered the door she was back downstairs.

'Hello, Carol. You finish clean?'

'Just finishing, M'am.'

'What's the matter girl, you look frightened?'

'Have a bad toothache M'am.'

'You should get them pulled, they just go cause you trouble.'

'Yes m'am.'

Shortly after, Legion came downstairs. He tried to act natural but he felt himself guilty.

'What's wrong you nose, boy?' Mother Frances asked, staring at him.

He hadn't noticed that he'd started to bleed again.

'Oh, I fell in the school yard.'

The answer seemed to satisfy them, but still there was something heavy in the air.

That evening at dinner, after Carol had gone, they seemed to be staring at him. His mother did not pay that much attention, but he could feel Mother Frances slowly piecing things together. He found his mind wandering.

'What's the matter, you not hungry tonight?'

'I hungry, yes.'

'You not eating much.'

'He must be need a dose of physic.'

They had given Carol a large parcel of clothes at the door when she was leaving and some extra money. He noticed the way she was looking at him.

When he went to bed that night he tried to imagine she was there with him. He could remember everything her body did, and the deep smell that she had. He could remember, too, the feeling of dizziness that had overcome him. He had never felt like that before. It frightened him, but he liked it.

He would have to wait until another time when they could be alone. He would eat as much as he could, and jump and run so he could grow faster for her. So she wouldn't say that it wasn't long enough yet.

Some of the boys would smoke cigarettes; they said it made your voice deeper and your whistle long.

Outside he could hear the crickets. He could smell the camphor balls they placed in his room to keep the moths away. And the eucalyptus which Mother Frances used against fever.

The darkness came down around him and pulled him into itself. He made a ball of his body to keep his warmth close. It made him think of Carol. He couldn't tell when it happened, but sleep came.

In the morning it rained hard and the sound of thunder woke him. It passed quickly and soon the cock was crowing and he knew it was early.

His nose was still sore and the fingers of his right hand ached where he must have been struck while trying to parry the blows. He didn't mind though. He just hoped she would hurry and come back.

She did not come back, though. She never entered the house again. He soon realized what the look she gave him had meant. And the parcel they gave her at the door. For weeks he would ask about her, but they never answered him. Then one day someone said she went off with some man she was making a baby for.

He had wanted more time but he couldn't get it now. Only a few minutes in the upper room between his bleeding and her laughter. He should have kept her panties with her smell. Something. But he had to make do with memory and rumour.

Because on the Island people disappear from girlhood into woman. They move further and further into the bush and are kept by babies and men with rum-voices and thick wrists and heavy hands that wield machetes.

He wanted to fight for her, but he could not find out who the enemy was or how to fight.

He heard Mother Frances say: 'Woman is going be that boy Kinna Root. They go nyam he.'

Jumbi Kinna, the word was African. She would speak patois with the older women. His mother couldn't even understand when they spoke together.

And the next woman leaned over to her and laughed. Legion could see their shadows flickering on the wall. The kerosene lamp made their bodies look ever more mysterious.

Mother Frances had money and possessions. She had been to big cities and other islands, yet when she tied her head and walked the hills you could not tell her apart from the others of the bush. There was town and there was bush, and Mother Frances was of the bush.

'Yes,' said the other.

'For true, woman is that boy Kinna. Just like he father. So it really be. Bad like salt.'

The words stayed in his mind as though burned in by fire. 'Woman is that boy Kinna, just like he father.' When he saw Solo the next day he decided to ask him. Legion was on his way home from school, he made certain to go the long way. He knew he would meet Solo, who always came along that road, driving the goats with a piece of jook. He didn't run up to Solo immediately. He took his time because he had to choose his words carefully; he didn't like to look ignorant to anyone, especially not Solo. He knew how to read and spell, but next to Solo he always felt backward. Solo watched him in silence for a while, then spoke:

'So you back to you school. What happen, them catch you out?'

'They catch me, yes.'

'So what them do?'

Legion looked away towards the goats. 'Nothing.'

'You too lie. Them must be cut you rass. They make you fart fire. I feel say, them must of lick you when I don't see you come back next day.'

'Is all right.'

'You want play hard but is soft you soft.'

He started to walk off. Legion walked behind him.

'Solo, tell me something?'

'Is what?'

'What Kinna mean?'

'Kinna?'

'Yes, me hear someone say that woman is Kinna. Bad like salt.'

Solo laughed. 'Kinna is poison, like when you eat something that not good for you.'

'They say woman was my father Kinna. But who is my father?'

'Me no know. Can't even self say who me father be, never mind yours.'

'But how them come to be father?'

'What the matter with you, you dottish?'

This was exactly what Legion didn't want to happen. Again he felt foolish before Solo, but he needed to know certain things and only Solo could tell him.

'Remember when Tall-boy top that girl down by the beach, when like a fool you give we away? Well, you see what he was doing, right?'

'You mean pussy?'

'Yes, pussy. That's how you come father.'

'You mean like what horse does do and cat?'

'Same way.'

Legion's eyes got wide. 'You mean that's how babies come?'

'Is how else you think they come? Is just so you born. Is what you mother do with you father.'

A sudden violent rage siezed Legion.

'No, no, is not so my mother do.'

'You mother spread she legs and hoist up she dress same way.'

In a second he was on Solo. The boy was a year older than him and much taller, but he couldn't stand the smile on the other's face.

'Never say that about me mother.'

Solo laughed and with two quick blows had Legion lying on the side of the road. Then Legion tried to wrestle him but this was useless. Solo spent every day in some fight or other against boys twice his size. Those he could not conquer with his fist he would go at with his slingshot, with which he had deadly accuracy. He didn't waste any energy on Legion. He merely flipped him backwards.

'You want dead or what?'

Legion made as if to get up and try again.

'Look, Legion, don't make me have for kill you right. Just lay there and rest yourself. Listen, is how you born, is how I born, is how everybody born. Now go way and learn some sense. Schoolboy. School got you chupid.'

Legion got up slowly and cleaned himself off. He gathered up his school books and watched Solo disappear around the bend of the road. Two of the goats had scattered when they had started fighting. Another had just stood there a half-quizzical look on its face and chewing grass.

Legion walked home slowly. If what Solo had said was true then a lot of things made sense. And yet it didn't seem possible somehow. He thought of the many times he had heard women gossiping about so and so making a baby for this or that man. Was that why girls disappeared?

And the most upsetting thing of all: what of his own

mother, had she too done this with a man? She must have. But who was this man? Mother Frances would know, but it would be impossible to ask her. The mention of such a thing was certain to bring down her wrath on him.

Still, he had to find out somehow. That evening he gave his mother a very cold stare. Every time he looked at her he did it. He felt betrayed. He had thought of her in a world quite different from his and Solo's and Tall-boy's. He had thought that the three of them had invented sex and were alone in that world of mystery which was under women's dresses. Now it seemed that everyone was doing it. It made it cheap and ordinary. And if his mother did it, then Mother Frances must have done it too, otherwise his mother could not have been born.

The trail led on and on and there were more and more conspirators. All of which led him to the ultimate question: Who was his father? Would he know him if he saw him? There must be some way to know. It would take time, but he would find out. He set his mind to it.

He remembered one day by the sea wall. He was with his mother, and she met a man. The man put Legion to ride on a donkey and gave him candy; and when the man touched him softly, he remembered she cried and they whispered together. Could that have been him — or did he dream it?

That had been his second moment of perfect clarity; he did not like that awakening. His first moment was when he saw Carol naked for the first time. The universe had been revealed to him then, he knew it, and he liked it. He could interpret the island through her body. Her breasts were the villages above the town. Between her thighs was the town itself at midday when the fierce heat fell and your body became weak and had to submit. The legs were the paths which collided with the town.

Now she would not come again and he would have to await the next awakening. He was angry with himself for not interpreting birth. He should have figured it out himself. If what Solo said was true then people were the same as animals they fed and beat. He remembered seeing two dogs in heat. The male climbed on the back of the bitch and started with his spasms, but all the while he seemed not to realize what he was doing. The look on his face was vacant, and yet they continued.

Solo had an advantage over Legion. He lived in the streets and slept in the makeshift houses of the village. The thin walls and shuttered windows were always filled with the sounds of orgasm and argument. Nothing could ever take place without the entire village knowing. Children knew everything the adults did and many times could anticipate better than their parents what would take place next. Solo lived with an aunt who was the only parent he knew. He seldom came home and she seldom looked for him. She had seven children of her own and his absence was well appreciated and often encouraged. He soon learned to steal whenever possible and to run. To eat alone, away from envious eyes, and never to let on how much money he had or where he got it. Solo would sleep with his cousins and do what he could with them until they pushed him away or the stink of urine-soaked mattresses was too much for him. He soon learned how many openings girls had to their bodies and lived secure with his knowledge.

Legion was different. He was an only child and, although the details of his birth were obscure, he knew from the earliest that he was very special. He was a boy child, the first in three generations.

Mother Frances liked to call him the prince. She would see to it that he had only the best and would not perish before his time. He wanted for nothing which could be bought. It was right that he should be spoiled because he had what few on the island had: a future.

Mother Frances had worked as a domestic abroad in Canada and America. She had a daughter, Dora, who was Desmie's mother, and Dora had married a man much older than herself. He died shortly after their marriage. They made only one child, Desmie. When Dora died too, Mother Frances honoured an old promise by bringing Desmie up and giving her her name. Her sister was still there working. Mother Frances had managed to save (together with her sister Annie) a large amount of money which, when converted into the island currency, was a fortune big enough to make her an aristocrat. Through the acquisition, sale and rental of land, Mother Frances had made her name and fortune: land, which had once been cheap and plentiful, was now the island's most precious commodity. Desmie had been sent to boarding school, there to master Latin and piano. She worked in the only bank for a time on her return and was encouraged to take up a post as schoolteacher. Teacher Biddy herself had recommended her as her successor. The idea had little appeal for the young girl though. She preferred instead to attend parties and work in the bank, which was a good vantage point from which she could see and be seen.

At eighteen she had but one deep ambition in life: to leave the island. The leaving of the island was every young person's dream, they talked of it quietly or yelled it when the frustration was unbearable.

There were five top families on the island. They tried to keep each other from mental collapse. They took turns going on trips to the larger islands, bringing back mementoes and small pieces of scandal. Each planned their escape, the women choosing marriage.

'Girl, I simply must leave this island before I die,' said Stephanie Simpson to Desmie one day in the garden as they listened to gramophone records.

'There is absolutely not a thing here for any civilized person to do, except . . . you know what.'

'I feel I'd like to try but Mother Frances would kill me.'

'She wouldn't have to know,' said Stephanie with a mischievous smile.

Desmie looked at her and laughed. She was Stephanie's closest friend. Yet that did not mean they trusted each other beyond a certain point. She had heard rumours of how Stephanie had aborted a baby when she was sixteen. Still, Stephanie had never admitted this or any other actual indiscretion. She would merely give hints.

Some had said of her that although Stephanie was born of a high-class family (which meant she had a toilet indoors instead of outside) she still had bad blood in her. She had a thirst for sex and although her family sent her to a good school, the only thing which the girl would study was man. The servants knew these things for they kept a better eye on their young mistress than her parents did.

It was Stephanie who would tease Desmie about her lack of experience. Desmie had been kissed many times and had even danced close with certain boys on special occasions, but that was the limit of her knowledge.

Whereas Stephanie had a certain freedom of movement, Desmie had none. Stephanie had a mother and father (he

was a judge and had been to England once); Desmie had
only Mother Frances who was more vigilant than a father
would be. Then, too, she had a score of friends who made it
their business to report to her Desmie's movements and
sightings of the young girl in any questionable company.

One day while Desmie was working in the bank, between
gossiping with another girlfriend, she noticed a young man
she had never seen before. He was well dressed and waited
deliberately for her to serve him. He smiled at her from out of
his silence and gave her a money order to be cashed. This
done, he thanked her, looked at her for a moment as if
making a decision, and then turned and left. The other girls
started to talk about how good-looking he was and how slick
the cut of his trousers.

'Did you see the way he was studying you, girl?'

'Me, I never noticed him,' said Desmie, sucking her teeth.

She thought no more of it until he returned three days
later. Again he waited especially for her to serve him. This
time he came to make a deposit. She accepted the bank book
and made the necessary inscriptions.

'May I ask your name, Miss?'

'And why you want to know my name?'

'Because I want to know you.'

'And suppose I don't want you to know me?'

'Well, I would have to accept that,' he smiled.

Half of her wanted to tell him her name, yet this was not
the way it was done on the island. Everything took its time
here, greetings, birth and death. She liked his smile, though,
and something about his manner: he had a certainty which
frightened her. She made discreet enquiries about him. She
was sure he had already done that about her; no doubt he

already knew her name and the fact that she was unattainable.

She soon learned why he attracted her and yet was frightening. Carlton Wade was a man of gentle manner and a passion for gambling and women. It was said of him that he had exceptional luck with cards and would think nothing of spending three days without seeing daylight, focusing only on a card table. He had many women and few commitments. He was a chief operator with the Cable and Wireless Company and was called upon when any dangerous job had to be done involving electricity. He also had a penchant for travel and would vanish for six months or a year with little notice to anyone.

'I see,' said Desmie. 'Carlton Wade, is it.'

She was not very surprised when the following week Carlton appeared as she was leaving work. He was spotlessly dressed in a white suit and had brought her flowers. She did not go with him but she accepted the flowers. This was the beginning of his campaign.

Three days a week he was there regularly to take her to lunch, each time making certain he was dressed differently. Then came the small gifts of silver bracelets and gold. Still he waited. She must be careful not to be seen with him in certain places without her girlfriends to chaperone her.

Carlton knew well how to make things comfortable and easy. He was very easy to like and quite comfortable to love. Since he knew of the difficulty of Desmie's position, he was particular where they would be seen together. He soon took to hiring cars to pick her up after work to take her for outings and meals. Gradually he grew bolder and started to rent houses where they could be alone together. This involved a lot of money, for first there was the cost of the house and then the employment of a cook and maid (who usually left before Desmie arrived), and finally a car and driver to fetch her.

The first time this plan was put into motion it failed miserably. The house and everything had been prepared but the driver was too talkative. As the car was approaching the rendezvous house, the driver turned to her and said:

'So you know Softcandle?'

Desmie, who was already feeling apprehensive, looked at him and said, 'Beg pardon?'

'Softcandle, you know, Carlton. That's how we call him.'

'Softcandle? . . . No, I don't know him very well.'

'But you going to meet him, no?'

'No, I think not. Please take me back.'

'What, you mean you want to go back to town? Look, we almost there.'

Desmie cleared her throat and said in her most authoritative voice, and with no trace of a doubt, 'I said take me back please. NOW.'

The driver looked at her face in the mirror and seeing the seriousness there, as well as the face that he'd said quite the wrong thing, tried again.

'Look, he's a very nice guy, Carlton. We all like him. I meself know him from small.'

'I'm quite sure he is very nice. Can you turn the car around please.'

The driver made an abrupt U-turn and drove back to the town. It was a long dusty way. When they arrived back in the centre he opened the door and let her out. He wanted to curse at her but knew better, so instead he said: 'All right now?'

'Fine, thank you.'

'And what must I tell Carlton?'

'Tell him I won't be coming today.'

With that she moved off with a graceful gait with just the slightest suggestion of a provocative twist of her bottom.

The driver realized that his news would not be gratefully received; he only hoped that Carlton would not take out his anger on the courier.

It being Friday, Carlton was unable to see her again until the following Monday, unless he felt bold enough to call upon her at her house. This he almost did but after hearing rumours of how Mother Frances kept watch there, he decided against this course of action.

That Monday morning he stormed into the bank. He went immediately over to the window where she worked.

'Is what you think you playing?'

Desmie met his gaze directly with no wavering.

'I don't think I'm playing at anything. I'm working and unless you have some business at this window I suggest you leave because people are staring.'

He looked about him and noticed the gossipy eyes of the tellers set on him. He reached in his pocket and withdrew some five dollar notes.

'I'm sorry, can you put this in my savings account?'

'Certainly sir, have you brought your account book with you?'

He fumbled in his jacket and found the book.

'Look, why didn't you come Friday? I had everything arranged.'

'I didn't like your driver, that's why.'

'Why not?'

'Because he talks too much. I think he's dangerous and besides. . .'

'Besides what?'

'I don't think I like your name.'

'My name?'

But she wouldn't explain any further. She merely handed him back his bank book.

Carlton Wade was not used to being rejected by a woman. Desmie now became an obsession. There were more and more gifts and more and more elaborate plans.

She knew well that the men of the island only liked two types of women: their mothers (or women of the age group beyond sex) and women whom they could not have. All the others were used and flung aside after conquest. Desire and hatred moved together in island men.

Drawn by desperation, he overcame his caution and came visiting one afternoon at the house of Mother Frances Barzey. He was careful of dress and soft of speech. He entered with hat in hand and kerchief at the ready, but he forgot to close the gate behind him. This Mother Frances noted, together with the fact that his shoes were too pointed and his smile too ready. He was not invited to stay for dinner but was given lemonade and a slice of cake. He was offered rum but the signal was given by Desmie that it was best not to accept it.

He was questioned gently and thoroughly about his family but could answer only as far back as one generation. He felt proud of the fact that he knew who his mother was. Mother Frances blinked twice and remarked that darkness would soon be falling. Realizing that this was a signal for him to take his leave, Carlton rose and smiled.

Desmie walked him through the garden and was soon called in by Mother Frances who had need of her.

Two kisses later, Carlton started the long descent to the village. The next day a young boy arrived at the house bearing a parcel which he gave to Mother Frances.

'Beg pardon, M'am, Mr Wade said I must bring this for you and would you please to accept this from him.'

Inside she found three ripe avocado pears. Mother Frances was impressed, but not impressed enough to accept this young suitor for her Desmie's hand and body. She soon made enquiries in the village. Within two days she knew all she needed to and more regarding Carlton Wade Esquire. She waited until dinner:

'Me hope to God you no deal with this damn scamp you know?'

'Who you talking about, Mother?'

'You know well enough who me talking bout. I talking bout you sweet man, Carlton. Me hear say the boy reckless. He done breed three gal them in a village, and have a next set in town. Him a scamp yes.'

'He's not a scamp, Mother.'

'What else you could call him but a damn scamp? You just make sure me don't hear nothing bout you and him. Don't bring no scandal me yard, mind what I tell you. Otherwise you fart fire.'

Desmie saw there was no use continuing this argument for they had come to a wall. There was no way to win except to curse and that would be beyond the boundary. Instead she cried, which was acceptable, for it meant that the old woman had won. The whole purpose of the exercise had been to reduce her to tears, which meant defeat.

Mother Frances had a much larger armoury of emotions to draw on when necessary, but for now age and intimidation were sufficient. the subject was not brought up again that evening, but in the morning Desmie saw her purposefully give away the avocados to one of the workers. She muttered: 'I don't know what kind of obeah the man might be put pon these things them.'

When Desmie saw that, she immediately made up her mind that she would let Carlton make love to her. She was not her grandmother's equal in confrontation but was certainly her match in will.

That day she chose her dress very carefully, as well as the underwear and perfume she would wear. When she arrived at work she got more than the usual number of compliments.

Carlton arrived at noon, as she knew he would. She was very casual in her tone.

He was both eager and anxious to know if the old woman had liked his little gift.

'What she say about the avocados?'

'She didn't . . . say very much you know.'

'You think she like me?'

'I don't think you should go back there again.'

'Well, what I must do, I want to see you?'

'Well, maybe if you send a car for me again, with a different driver this time, I might come.'

She said this without looking at him.

'A car soon come.'

He tried to look cool but she could see he was nervous. He had a lot to prepare, but by afternoon, when she finished working, the car was ready to take her. This driver said nothing and kept his eyes on the road.

When she arrived at the house she could see the place was well cleaned. Dinner had been prepared and left for them. There was a victrola and radio and several bottles of drink.

They ate and talked about everything except the large double bed which she knew would be waiting upstairs. She did not drink anything and kept staring at him, which made him feel uneasy. This was not going to be an easy conquest like the mindless shopgirls from the bush he was accustomed to. He could not get her drunk quickly. He would have to talk, there was no way of avoiding it.

She watched him as he tried to visualize the attack in his mind, as though, by thinking, to bring it into existence. She crossed her legs as he finished his third glass of rum. He was about to pour himself another when she stopped his hand midway in the action and told him not to. She drew him over beside her on the couch and let him kiss her once and then twice. She felt his heart starting to race and saw the throbbing in his trousers. He went to press her to the sofa.

'I think it's time for me to go now, Carlton.'

'What?' A look of utter shock had appeared on his face. 'You can't go now.'

'Do you ever want me to come back again?'

'Yes.'

'Well then, I must go now.'

She gave him another kiss by the door and his hand started to roam along the smoothness of her skin. The dress she wore was of fine cotton and the heat of her body came through to him. If it were any other girl he would have known what to do, but this one made him feel uncertain.

'All right, I'll wait, but if you don't come back I go to you Mama yard and catch you.'

She could see he meant it.

The car took her close to her gate.

Three days later she returned again. This time she stayed late.

She would not let him drink any more before he made love to her. She did not like the smell of it on his breath. She teased him and asked him if he needed it to make him come big. He took the challenge and made love to her without it. He was gentle at first; he didn't want to frighten her away, but he could see soon that she took it as a very serious thing, making love. She would never let him hurry. He soon learned her rhythm.

Their meetings became regular. The lies to Mother Frances more bold. There were times when she almost wanted her to know what she was doing. She would have liked to bring him home one night and dare her. The island had life for her now only when she was in his house and he was breathing inside of her. Then she could forget the painful slowness of the place, the vacant faces and pointless conversations, and all the disease of the small island mind. It was as if he brought her from the sleep of the grave which they called existence but she knew to be death.

One night she was sleeping in her room upstairs and she heard the sound of pebbles at her window shutters. She covered herself and went out hoping. She had not seen him for two weeks. She wondered if his desire had cooled. She couldn't believe he was bold enough to come there to her house. They spoke in whispers and she kept straining to listen for Mother Frances' footsteps.

'What you do, you mad? How you could come here?'

'I want see you.'

She could smell that he had been drinking. She should send him away quickly before he was discovered and that would be the end; but she couldn't. Instead, she took him quickly inside to the laundry room of the house, the place furthest from her grandmother's room. She would have liked to take him upstairs to her bed because she had long dreamt of it, but her room was right next door to the old woman's and she dare not. She spread some towels and sheets on the floor and pulled him down beside her. Every time she wanted to scream out she bit into his shoulder. Their love-making had never been as intense before; it must have been the danger of being discovered at any moment. Or perhaps the fact that she had dreamt of having him like this here so many times. It was hard for her to send him away before dawn. She knew Mother Frances rose to say her prayers at first light. She saw him move away into the half darkness and tried to rid the house of all trace and scent of him. But most of him was in her.

For the next week Desmie went about with a strange glow. An outward and visible sign of an inward spiritual grace. Mother Frances soon noticed it and called it for what it was: brazenness. She would have confronted Desmie but there was nothing tangible upon which she could challenge her. Nonetheless the glow was definitely there.

Desmie went about the house touching things and smiling

to herself. She touched the table and thought to herself: 'He made love to me here.'

She walked into the laundry room and could feel his presence still. She ran her fingers along the back of the chair where he had sat. Her mind tempted her to bolder acts. She wanted to invite him back to exorcise the many demons which she knew were in the very walls of the house, causing it to suffocate anything which was young and natural. She now felt that the entire island was like that. Thick and putrid with the stench of the old and the dying. She looked at the young girl Annie, who was the housekeeper who came three times a week to scrub and polish. The girl was only fifteen, yet already she had the premature sadness of sickrooms and candles. She had spent too much time around the old women. Had never known a man and was not likely to. She always wore head-scarves because her hair had ceased to grow. Her hands were calloused and she had a nervous old woman's walk. A sort of half skipping motion which perfectly mirrored her mind.

Desmie saw in Annie everything she wanted to avoid being in life. A Seventh Day Adventist girl who was made for labour and caring for the sick. She wondered what Annie would do if she had caught her with Carlton. If her eyes had witnessed them climbing a passion peak. If Annie had seen her losing control and all consciousness passing from her eyes.

Desmie looked up from her reverie and noticed Mother Frances staring at her.

'But girl, what's wrong with you at all?'

'Wrong with me, Mother? Nothing, nothing is wrong with me. Why?'

'All I see you doing is smiling to yourself, and touching up yourself and laughing, like when people see duppy.'

Desmie wanted to burst out laughing but thought better of it.

'Nothing wrong, I was just thinking of a joke somebody tell me at work today, that's all.'

But she could see Mother Frances didn't believe her.

The only one Desmie could talk to now was Stephanie. She alone could understand what Desmie was feeling. The two girls would sit about on the patio and laugh to themselves.

'You fancy him, Desmie?'

'Yes.'

'What kind of lover he is?'

'I can't tell you that, girl.'

'Come on, tell me no. He look well fit.' (Much laughing and giggling.)

'He's all right, you know.'

'But he does hurt you.'

'No, he don't hurt me really.'

'I like a man hurt me.'

'Stephanie, you too damn reckless, girl.'

'I know, girl, what I could do. I was just born so.'

'When I'm with him I feel reckless,' said Desmie, looking off in the distance at some fireflies.

'Mother Frances know you still see him?'

'You mad?'

'You know what's wrong with this island, Desmie?'

'It too damn small.'

'That's right,' said Stephanie. 'Small island, small minds.

There's nowhere to go and nothing to do. You're lucky, at least you have a new man. I'm done with all of them from here. I can't wait for the Christmas holiday.'

'You going to go away again?'

'Most naturally. I'm going to spend the Christmas in Barbados.'

'But how you get to go away so much, girl?'

'My family prefers to have me away rather than cause them scandal here at home. They know I can't go more than six months without . . . something new.'

They laughed together and heard the echo of their voices break the brittle stillness of the night.

Desmie started to formulate her plans for the coming Christmas season. She wanted to do something wild and impulsive like Stephanie. She suggested to Carlton that they go away together for two weeks in Barbados. She would tell her grandmother that she was invited by Stephanie and her parents. Once there they could spend as much time together as they wanted. Carlton agreed that the idea was a good one. His only problem was money. He assured her that he was on a good winning streak now and that by serious application he would have enough within a fortnight's time. That would give them enough time as it was now the second week of November.

Desmie's mind came alive with expectation. She saw them together on the beach by moonlight. Saw them ordering food from room service and spending days together in bed. Most of all, she saw them free from prying eyes and the suffocation of their island. It was all so simple. This would be a test period. Who knows, if she found they could get on well together, perhaps they would never even bother to come back. She found herself laughing and singing to herself. Her workmates in the bank noticed and started to tease her;

'Something sweet you, Desmie?'

'But look at the girl. Eh eh, is bright she bright.'

'Never see she so happy. Is who holding you hand?'

She paid them no mind. They knew they were trapped there. Stuck to the flypaper of their existence with no hope save marriage, childbirth and death. They would repeat their parents' lives and drink themselves into senility when reality became too much for them. She would have liked to tell them how foolish they really were and what a poppyshow. How many of the girls she had grown up with had become old before their time. How many had gone mad so as not to face the blows which their husbands gave them daily. The confrontations and gossip. When all became too much they would stand up in the middle of the church and confess to imagined sins and surrender to the blonde images of Christ which adorned the walls, the fans and the inside flyleaves of bibles.

'Poppyshow!' thought Desmie. 'One big mummer's play of foolishness.' She would not end up like this. Let them act out their rituals, clean their fish in dirty little shanty houses. Beat their children and wait for death. She at least would escape. The thought filled her with pleasure and made the waiting bearable.

The prospect of the rendezvous in Barbados put her life in perspective. Stephanie was now her closest friend. She had studied abroad in England and attended boarding school there. Whereas Desmie was from the monied nouveau riche, Stephanie was from the long-established elite which on the island meant merely having come from two generations of money instead of one. There were always parties at Stephanie's house and friends were always sleeping over. One Friday, Desmie spent the weekend there together with another girl, Rita. They had been drinking apricot brandy and gossiping into the small hours of the morning. Because the brandy liqueur tasted sweet, Desmie did not fear its potency but she soon noticed that she was pleasantly drunk. After a time she went off to the guest-room which she often used when she stayed over at Stephanie's. She went to bed soon after but found she couldn't sleep. The noise of the crickets outside sounded much louder to her for some reason. Perhaps it was the strange bed or the fact that Stephanie lived in a different part of the island. She decided to go and ask Stephanie for some of her magazines from America. *True Romance* magazines were Stephanie's favourite, together with *Hollywood Stars*.

Desmie entered the hallway and made her way quickly to Stephanie's room. She did not want to awaken Stephanie's parents, although she could hear the heavy snoring of the father. When she reached Stephanie's door she could hear voices. The door was ajar and she assumed they were still talking. As she made to open the door and call the girl's name, she was suddenly shocked to find the two girls in an embrace. Desmie had never seen anything like this before. She stood stunned and unable to speak as she saw them kissing and playing with each other's breasts. Only once before had she heard of this strange kind of goings-on. It was rumoured that a cousin of theirs was a 'bulla' woman. A woman who liked other women. This cousin, whose name was Stella, was a very hard-looking woman who liked doing carpentry and house painting. It was said of her that she was as strong as any man on the island, if not stronger. With cousin Stella it was indeed plausible that she should like women. From her appearance one could easily imagine the rumours to be true. It was merely an accident of nature which made Stella a woman anyway. She was surely meant to be a man.

But Stephanie, who had all the mystique of womanhood and upper class sensibility about her, was quite another matter. She saw the girl lift Stephanie's dress and start to kiss her on her thighs. 'No,' thought Desmie, 'this couldn't be happening.' But Stephanie made no attempt to stop the girl; she welcomed her and started to gasp and cry out the same way Desmie did with Carlton.

She turned and tried to make her way quietly back to her room. She just made it inside when her stomach started to heave. She ran to where she knew the posy was stationed beneath the bed and threw up violently for some time. The apricot brandy no longer tasted sweet.

She lay on the bed and tried to reason. The world in one quick-blinding revelation no longer made sense. The feeling of harmony she had felt suddenly distorted itself and looked like the multicoloured vomit she had just heaved from her body. Why, she asked herself, why should a girl like Stephanie who had everything, men, money and education, do something so perverse? There was, she knew, sickness in the world. She knew there was such a thing as mental as well as physical sickness, but she only saw it manifest itself in the kind of madness which left people screaming at the moon. There were definitely many mad people on the island. This she had known, but all the mad people had been given a special name identifying both their malady and their station in life. Like the fellow they called Hopping Dick who used to appear on a crowded street without his pants on, apparently totally unaware of his state. There was Mad Mary who would talk to spirits. Such mad people were common enough and in most cases there was a good reason. The death of a wife, or being abandoned by a man, which drove them to that state. What could be said about Stephanie? She had everything. Or maybe she wasn't mad, thought Desmie. Maybe I'm the one that is mad. I could never let another woman do that to me. The thought of it made her want to vomit again but nothing came up this time.

Desmie tried to make some sense of it but abandoned it after a while, coming to no clear conclusion. She thought of perhaps leaving the house immediately. Not waiting for morning. But then what excuse could she give? If Stephanie ever suspected that she knew, Desmie would have made an enemy for life. A very dangerous enemy for she had foolishly confided in Stephanie many things about Carlton and their affair. If Stephanie said anything to Mother Frances, the trip to Barbados would certainly be cancelled. No, she could not leave the house yet. She had to stay and endure until the morning. By then she would think up some politic excuse for leaving and not staying the weekend.

She tried to relax. Her mouth felt bitter from the after-taste of her sickness. Eventually, as dawn came on, she drifted into the unconsciousness of sleep.

She saw herself at Carnival. The first day, Ju vais, of

Carnival, when the men dress up as women. The scene frightened her. She wanted to escape. She was looking everywhere for Carlton but all the strange, night-faced people blocked her. She ran through the crowded street and came upon some mummers dressed in bright robes. They were playing mento music. One man had a fife. She thought it was Carlton and reached for the mask which he wore but as she reached up the man slapped her and she saw it wasn't Carlton. She found herself running until she came to the sea, which frightened her because the waters were so rough. She had to turn back. Then a fat woman came up to her and tried to kiss her. She could not push her away and the woman's breath smelled of rum and tobacco like a man's. Suddenly there was a group of women. They encircled her. She felt herself suffocated by their embrace but she could still hear the sea raging. She called out for her mother, who approached in a long white dress. The dress was embroidered and she wore a veil. She called her mother's name again but as the woman approached she saw that it was not Dora.

She was screaming but the others took no notice of her screams. They started instead to pull off her clothes and she knew what they wanted to do with their fingers. She was starting to vomit now and when they saw her they stepped back. The woman in white came forward and bent over her. She smelled of lime and the linament rub which her mother used on her chest.

The woman wiped Desmie's face with the veil she wore and then started to roll her towards the sea. Over and over she rolled down into the deepness of the foaming water. With that, Desmie cried out once more and heard voices over her.

The voices became one voice and she realized it was Stephanie's mother calling down to her.

'Child, you all right? You having a nightmare?'

Desmie looked up and realized where she was. She apologized for waking her. She sat up in bed and stared out into the morning mist which came down from the Soufriere volcano. She was alone now, trembling. Then she was still. Like a lamp in a windless place.

THE SEASON OF EXPECTATION

Christmas came upon the island. It was expected and yet sudden. Desmie had given Mother Frances warning of her plans to spend the two weeks in Barbados with her friend Stephanie. She had made preparations a month in advance. Her clothes were made ready and her ticket purchased.

Everywhere on the island the radios sang out Bing Crosby's 'White Christmas' which, although it was absurd in the heat and humidity of the islands, still brought smiles to sweaty black faces. There was even mistletoe and a Christmas tree set up in the bank where Desmie worked.

People stocked up on pork and spirits so that they wouldn't be caught short. There were rude assignations made and some accepted, for Christmas was a randy season on the island. Christmas meant carnival and marching bands which would go from house to house in an endless fete of food, dancing and music. Many people would simply stop work a week before Christmas and never return until well into the New Year. There was a desperation and a madness about Christmas. It was generally accepted that this was what life was all about. It made the rest of the ordinary year bearable.

Desmie kept mostly to herself. She did not mind the rude jokes and the bold overtures which she quite expected. She would merely smile and parry, for she knew what she was waiting for, with all the beating of her heart. She would get away from this dull island and have her tryst with her man Carlton. She dare not say his name aloud. Two weeks in Paradise.

'I'm dreaming of a White Christmas.'

She found herself unwillingly singing the song. She had seen the film at the cinema. She could not comprehend the snow but everything looked right. The horsedrawn carriage. The sleighbells ringing, and especially the two lovers in each other's arms. She asked her grandmother about America. She wanted to know what life was like there. Was it like the film? Yes, it must be. And what did snow feel like?

'Strange,' was all the old woman said, in a very non-committal voice.

She had worked for fifteen years as a domestic for a white family in Canada and then in the States. Of these years Desmie could learn little. There were photographs of Mother Frances and her sister in various poses. In some they wore elaborate hats. One in particular Desmie noted. Her grandmother was in a black uniform and wore an apron. She seemed quite proud in that photograph. In another she stood with her sister in a large winter coat. They were holding two white children by the hand. These children were in their charge.

'Well, I'll be leaving next week,' said Desmie.

The old woman gave her a wide-eyed look.

'Leaving?'

'Of course, next week, for Barbados, remember?'

'Oh, I don't think so,' she said.

Desmie was shocked. She felt her voice breaking and she made an effort not to scream.

'What do you mean, you don't think so? I told you over a month ago.'

'I getting old, girl. I does forget things now you know. Anyhow, no need to shout, I can hear you.'

Desmie wanted a confrontation. Something to bring this to a head. She had waited so long for this Christmas. The first chance she would have to be with Carlton for days together. To sleep with him, to wake with him. To not have to hide and sneak about. To not have to leave him just when their love making was starting to have a rhythm. No, she would not give this up easily. But her grandmother was more subtle. She would have no confrontation. Just a word here, a pause there. A walk to the window. A distracted search for some lost article of clothing.

'Now where I put that slip?'

'I've already bought my ticket.'

'What ticket you talking?'

'My boat ticket.'

'Well, Desmie, you know I'm not feeling too well these days and I would have thought you'd be here at Christmas with me. Christmas not a time to travel, girl. You should be with your family.'

The old woman could sense passion. She could not identify it by name but somehow she could sense that the girl was up to something that smelled of passion.

'Is who you going with on this trip?'

'I told you, Stephanie.'

'Stephanie mother go let she go way at Christmas?'

'Yes.'

'Well, she people always strange anyway.'

The following day she came down with a severe attack of shortness of breath and had to spend the day in bed. The doctor was called and various purgatives given. There was certainly no way to diagnose this symptom with any degree of certainty. The illness was just vague enough to cause concern and attention. Had Mother Frances simply said no, there would have been the confrontation which Desmie wanted badly. But no such refusal came. West Indians never say no. As such the burden was now on Desmie. The burden of guilt. Could she simply leave her grandmother in such a condition and go off with her lover in this Christmas season? And if she died, how could she ever sleep again in that house or even on that island? Already word was spreading quickly among the old women that Mother Frances was feeling poorly and may not live to see the New Year in. Wherever she went people would question Desmie about the state of Mother Frances' health. Friends began to converge on the house like predatory birds. With each solicitous enquiry Desmie saw her dreams of escape become dimmer.

Could anyone take her place at the bedside? No, Mother Frances would not stand for that. She made the feeling of guilt all the worse by steadfastly refusing help.

'Oh no, dear, you go on with your holiday. I don't want any stranger staying in me house over the Christmas.'

At last Desmie accepted defeat. There would be no holiday. Upon hearing this, Mother Frances started on the slow road to recovery. She was able to be up and about enough to fix the Christmas dinner. It was at this point that Desmie knew clearly that she had been used. The resentment grew to hatred. Hatred soon passed to resolution.

All right then, if she could not go away with her man at Christmas she would surely have him right there on the island.

She became ruthless. She not only slept with him at his house but now set about wilfully to have him in her own. She knew she was being reckless but she did not care now.

As the people ate their roast pork and drank strong bush rum, she set about her plan. She would sneak him in by night. Right there in her grandmother's house. She would have to be careful now that they were not found out. Of late, her mother had purchased a guard dog. He was set loose at night. There had been talk of thieves who came in search of chickens. Although they had not been robbed, Mother Frances took the precaution. Somehow Desmie felt that there was more than a fear of burglary behind this new acquisition. She could not help but wonder if perhaps her mother had heard her with Carlton when he had come once before by night. She would not put it past the old woman to have either seen or sensed that a man had been there.

Desmie did not care. Somehow she would have this victory. Here on this airless island, with too many old women with their smell of medicine and lamentations. This island which sucked life from the young and abandoned them to senility and gossip.

Carlton could not understand why she wanted him to come there. It did not make sense. It was one thing for him to have come that night when he was drunk and in heat. But now this was quite another thing when she summoned him there. It was more calculated and dangerous with the guard dog. Still, there was no accounting for a woman's moods. He thought to himself: one moment they're full of fear and modesty, and the next brazen as soldiers.

The operation was carried out with military skill. The dog was given bush rum in his food and was soon in a drugged sleep. He had howled for some time, which caused Mother Frances to remark: 'But what wrong with that blasted dog?'

When he finally fell off into his drugged sleep, Desmie left the gate open for Carlton. Her heart started racing again as she waited.

He was late. Why was he late? Was he gambling or was he with another woman? If he dared to see another woman first then she would surely know. She would be able to tell by the smell of cheap perfume which would cling to his body. Few women on the island had any taste in perfume. They would buy it as cheaply as possible and then use too much in an effort to overcome the stench of sweat. No, he could not possibly be so foolish as to see another woman first. But this was Christmas and men did foolish things.

Desmie could hear the music coming from houses in the distance. It mingled with the sound of laughter. Perhaps he was nearby now. Some churches were holding late services in a desperate attempt to win away some souls from carnival. There was always a struggle between good and evil, but the battle was especially heated during Carnival. Certain ministers became more vigilant against the madness of orgy and drink which was the fete. It was one thing to stand in the pulpit and command the people not to join in the 'jump up'. To make them obey was quite another.

There were late night services which lasted until after midnight with much thumping of bibles and shaking of tambourines. Then a service again at dawn.

Desmie listened from her bedroom window. It was hard to distinguish between the sound of the church and the sounds of the party revellers. Mother Frances started to snore in the room next door to Desmie's. She had wanted to attend the candlelight service, but thought it more prudent to await the sunrise. It would not do for one who was supposedly close to death's door to be seen too active, even in the service of God.

Desmie listened for the sound of footsteps. There was no danger of her falling asleep. She thought of him entering and her thighs became wet inside. The sheet which covered her began to stick to her body, so she cast it off.

The anticipation was great. It gave her more pleasure than if he were there himself. It was an eagerness and an anxiousness. The fear of being caught made it even more exciting somehow. Her mind started to think of Stephanie, her girlfriend. There was now a kind of silent conspiracy between the two. She knew she could only trust her friend so far and no more. Yet it would be a comfort to be able to confide in someone about what she was feeling this night. Of course, she would tell Carlton, but a man could not really understand. He would feel only conquest, nothing more complicated.

There was a stirring at the gate. Her stomach felt tense. She leapt from the bed and looked from her window. Yes, she could make out his outline. It was him. Oh God, don't let the dog bark.

She moved silently down the stairs. For the first time she heard voices within the walls. Voices like duppy spirits. She hoped they would not tell on her. She challenged them:

'You've taken away my holiday but you won't take my joy this night, I tell you that.'

She opened the door to him and put her fingers to his lips to silence him and at the same time to prove to herself that he was really there.

He entered nervously but half laughing at himself. He did a pantomime of tiptoeing. He was lucky that he was not too large or awkward. He was five foot seven and had an easy carriage. He could sense his way about in the dark. She mocked him:

'You must be do this many times before.'

'Is why you say that?' he whispered back to her.

She took him into the laundry room and lay him down on a quilt she had placed there. He took off his shoes and then started to stroke her softly.

He was not certain whether to undress her first or start to undress himself. He decided not to worry about it but let things take their own direction. He realized that it was her request that he be there. She did not want him to undress. She wore only the thin nightdress and it was easy and so soft beneath him that soon he found himself tearing at it.

She unzipped him and made him enter her first there, but only for a minute. Soon she stopped him and made him follow her into the living room. There again she made him enter her. Then she led him upstairs to her room.

As he passed the old woman's room he could hear her snoring soundly. 'Well, that's all right then,' he thought. 'Just make she stay so and everything well nice.'

They entered her room and there she finally let him undress. He made certain to place his clothes carefully in a single place so as to be able to collect them quickly if need be.

All jewellery (the gold ring and chain he wore) he placed inside his shoe.

Now he climbed into bed beside her and they started the rhythm. Slowly at first but the desperation came after. The anger, the hopelessness. And the walls which now said: 'No, you can't have him.' And the ceiling which called out her name: 'Desmie, what you doing?' And the window which said: 'We go catch you, girl. Make you stand before preacher.'

He was coming inside her, but really she was coming inside him. And when she came up to meet him it was a challenge and a confrontation. The one she could not have with her grandmother. The one which was always beneath the surface of things. He cupped his hands beneath her to keep her steady because now she seemed to be running ahead of him. The race was at her tempo. There was a clearing which she was bound for and at times she would not wait for him. Her legs were longer than his and so could entwine him as a vine.

He stilled her: wait. He used his strength but she used her need.

A mad thought came to her. She would have liked to take him into Mother Frances' room and make love to him there on the floor beside the bed. Even now she wanted to scream out but dare not. The wanting to, the having to scream out and yet not being able to, made her even more excited.

He stopped for a moment and looked down into her face. The gesture was realization. It came to him that this was no ordinary passion she wanted from him tonight. It was not *from* him that she wanted but *through* him. He caught his breath and then followed her again.

He moved with her and together they *journeyed*

throughout the island and all the history of the island.

The annoyance of her first refusal. There were many meetings and many places they had seen together. Now they saw them again.

He ran ahead of her now, his own recollections of what he thought when he first saw her walking. The long graceful slow gait which was arrogant yet restrained. And how he had wanted. And now, here, this eve of Christmas. And her breathing hard beneath him and then it was coming. He forced down with pain and entered a softness and she swallowed him deeper than he had ever been.

She started to scream out, so he moved his shoulder over her mouth to stifle her scream and she bit him hard and swallowed him more. To a point from which he thought there was no resurrection. But there was.

When they came together her screams became lost in the restless sounds of the house's breathing. The floorboards of the house groaned. The scraping of the trees' branches against the window. Her heart was racing not only because she had reached the place where she wanted to be taken by him, but because now she could not trust herself. Had her screams awakened her grandmother? She wanted to be caught, to be found out, and yet she feared it. In her boldness she had taken him right to her own room. Just a thin wall away from where the old woman slept. She listened. Nothing. Could she really have slept through that last orgasm? For an instant another mad thought ran through her mind. What if the old woman was dead? That would be horrible. She would be cursed surely for even thinking it.

She half pushed him away from her, but soon pulled him back again.

They slept for a time then. Only fifteen minutes but long

enough to dream. She dreamt that they were together in a field and he was flying a kite which had many colours of red and gold and he held it by a long string, but the string was tangled. And then Mother Frances appeared and said that it wasn't right for a grown man to be playing with a kite like a child. And she began to argue with her but then the string was suddenly encircling her thighs beneath her dress and her grandmother bent over her and she smelled of Limacal and eucalyptus. Mother Frances started to pull at the string until she found where it was hidden beneath her dress: started to strike her with one hand and with the other she pulled at the string. Desmie woke then, still frightened, but instead of her grandmother's hand between her thighs she found his.

As the first light of dawn came on she made him dress and go. He checked about the room to make certain he did not leave anything. He had taken off his gold chain because she said it scratched her.

As she led him to the door they did not speak a word but used gestures and touches the way the deaf and dumb do.

As he walked slowly away from the house and towards the road he felt proud of his accomplishment. He had used her body well, proud of the goatish smell of his clothes, but as he walked along, the image of her face and the expression in her eyes came on him. It was a peculiar look which she gave him and it would take some time to decipher. It was not a look of timidity or fear she gave him. It was something else.

It was only later that he decided that it was she who was in control.

February came suddenly, shaking the island earth with storms which came easterly. Men found themselves waking from the alcoholic haze of Christmas and into the chill of poverty. Some who swore that they would stay drunk until the next Christmas found that they had no money to fulfil the threat.

Desmie felt inside herself that things were not quite right. It was at work in the bank one day that she suddenly had the first attack of nausea. She fought hard against it because she had a dislike of sickness. Still, eventually she had to excuse herself and run to the toilet. Her girlfriends said she must have caught a virus. It must be the uncertainty of the weather. They all told stories of other girls who had 'caught a draught' by night.

But her nausea became more constant and she could not help but notice the dizziness which sometimes overtook her when she walked. Probably a virus, she thought, it will pass. But her breasts became very sore and started to swell. Then she could no longer avoid the recurring fear in her mind.

'I'm pregnant.'

There were many calypsos and jokes about young girls who started to swell. None of them seemed funny to her now. People seemed to be eyeing her strangely. The men said that the bit of weight seemed to do her good and made her look more ripe, but the women whispered.

Finally, Desmie knew that she would have to seek advice. She knew that it was only a matter of time before she would have to face her grandmother's inquisition. She went to see Stephanie.

She had not been very close with her friend since that night when she found her in bed with another girl. She still liked Stephanie but she also feared her. Still, Stephanie was the only one whom she could trust. The other girls were too gossipy and foolish.

Stephanie had returned from Barbados and wore her hair in a new style. It made her look older. They sat together sipping tea in the garden. Stephanie's aunt had made ice cream in a bucket which tasted so good Desmie had to struggle with herself not to take a third helping.

'Stephanie, what if someone was pregnant?'

'Someone like who?'

'Just someone.'

Stephanie looked straight at Desmie and then just the slightest trace of a wicked smile appeared on her face.

'Well, that can be nice if that someone was married and had a nanny to see to the little beast.'

'But what if. . .'

'We had better go up to my room, don't you think, Desmie?'

Stephanie gave a conspiratorial nod of her head and Desmie followed her inside.

'What do you plan on doing now, Desmie?'

'I don't know.'

'Well, you better know fast. You're going to get married, of course?'

'I don't know.'

'Stop saying you don't know.'

'I'm confused.'

'You more pregnant than confused.'

Desmie picked up one of Stephanie's *True Romance* magazines which lay on the bed.

'Don't bother to look in there, it won't help you.'

'Aren't there things you could take?' Desmie asked without looking up from the magazine.

'You mean things like disinfectant or lye? They can kill you, girl.'

'But I've heard of things that women sell which can —'

'Bush medicine, obeah.'

'Something to bring down the baby.'

'You could take a chance, I guess.'

'It never happened to you, Stephanie?'

'No, girl. I make him come out when he's coming.'

Desmie started to blush.

'Me too, I make him come out, but sometimes it feel so —'

'So good.' Stephanie laughed.

'Don't laugh, girl, this is serious.'

'You should make him put something on if you can't stop.'

'He doesn't like to use things.'

Stephanie took the magazine away from her.

'Have you told him as yet?'

'No.'

'Oho, well you should. Make him marry you. Does he have money?'

'Sometimes.'

'Only sometimes? Oh my God, you are in trouble. What will you do if Mother Frances finds out?'

'Girl, I just dead.'

Stephanie walked about the room. Evening was falling.

'How many months are you?'

'Two I think.'

The figure two did not of itself seem very large. If, for example, she had said, I have two sins. Yet Stephanie seemed to take the news very gravely. To ease the weight of the silence Desmie added: 'I'm sure it's not more than two months.'

Stephanie sat beside her on the bed.

'Well, they say that there's a kind of bush tea you can take.

Bitter aloes tea. They say that it brings on the period.'

Desmie looked slightly bewildered.

'But this tea, it could stop pregnancy?'

'Well, so they does say, I can't be sure. Anyway, we could try Mrs Samuels.'

Desmie touched Stephanie's arm.

'But this Mrs Samuels, she does like to run she mouth too much.'

'But it she who keep the roots.'

'But if news reach me mother's ears I dead one time.'

Stephanie pulled a face. 'So if you don't get something soon she can see for she self, not so, Desmie?'

'I don't like troubling Mrs Samuels. She too fast in people business.'

Stephanie seemed to be growing tired of the subject. She had made suggestions and Desmie seemed intent on not following. Stephanie did not like to be contradicted.

'Well, tell your man, make him do something for you, after all is his fault.'

Desmie didn't answer. She realized that sooner or later she would have to confront him with the news. She did not want to appear to be begging him for anything. Most important of all, she must not appear to be hysterical like other girls she had heard of. She was not a peasant girl. She was of a higher class than he. You must never go down to people's level, you must bring them up to yours. She could hear the voice of her old schoolteacher, Teacher Biddy. The way the old spinster would smooth out her skirt and steady her voice before delivering some strong homily: the world is unclean and yet we must be clean. This is the burden of all well brought up young ladies, for you were not dragged up,

Desmie, you were brought up.

That evening she wrote a small message in her beautifully neat handwriting:

Dear Carlton,
Must see you tomorrow. I would like to speak with you. Please meet me after work.
                    Love always,
                    Desmie

She thought of adding 'important' or 'urgent' but decided against it, not wanting to frighten him away. She posted the letter and waited to see what would happen. That night she slept without dreaming.

The next day Desmie chose her dress carefully. She wanted something light and yet not too revealing. She decided on a blue cotton dress. She had worn it only once before and at that time it was a little large for her. Now it fitted easily. She wanted to be careful not to telegraph her secret too quickly to him. She wanted to feel him out. Would he come, though? Yes, of course he would come. She was not a nuisance to him as yet. She was still in charge of the relationship and allowed him to see her only at certain intervals.

She found herself very nervous at work. She made several errors in accounting at the bank and had to constantly re-check herself. The morning seemed to be dragging on.

He came at half-past eleven. It made her quite uncomfortable to see him there. She would not be able to speak with him now. She had wanted him to come at closing time. He seemed quite sure of himself. He wore a light grey suit; the lapels and sharp creases of his trousers gave him a very angular appearance. He did not bother with the sham of having come on business. He came very purposefully towards her window and made it quite evident that he came only to see her.

She kept an air of unconcern at seeing him. Her distance cut into him and made him annoyed. He had an unlit cigar in his hand which he seemed to have little intention of smoking. She decided it was for effect only.

'Thought you wanted to see me.'

'Not now, I'm very busy. You'll have to meet me after work.'

He smiled at her, not wanting to exit too quickly for he knew eyes were watching him.

'I have something for you, you know. Guess what it is.'

He reached inside of his jacket pocket to withdraw something but made a meaningful pause there for maximum attention.

She half looked up for a second and then replied: 'Not now, after work.'

He felt himself dismissed. He did not like it. He was accustomed to office girls abandoning their work the minute he entered. 'No', he thought, 'I still haven't conquered her yet. Not completely, but soon now. . .'

'All right, meet you at Dyers.'

He made a careful turn which was almost military. He did not want to seem foolish. He then gave a casual wave to a fellow who was doing business at one of the counters.

Desmie watched him exit from the corner of her eye. She did not want to lift her head from her work and possibly signal that his visit was of any importance to her. She was certain that she was being watched. She was always being watched.

The rest of the day she prepared the scene of their meeting in her mind. She knew just what mood she wanted to adopt. She rehearsed the order of the conversation. She would make it as vague as possible. Mislead him with several false starts and maintain a distant and slightly vacant look, more mysterious than vacant.

She could not help laughing at the uncertainty which she had already caused him. The way he did not seem to know what to do with his cigar. She would put him on the defensive by casually asking him midway through the conversation (and apropos of nothing which had gone before), 'So you really have no intention of ever staying with any one woman?' He certainly wouldn't know how to answer that. Then she would say in her most matter-of-fact voice: 'By the way, I think I'm pregnant.' She wouldn't say it to him in the restaurant. She would wait until they were walking along the road. She would wait and let him try to get her to visit his house — as he surely would — then she would tell him. Should she first go to the house and then tell him? Perhaps. She was undecided on that. She would see how she felt in the restaurant. Of course he would merely think that she was being moody. He often said that she changed moods as often as she changed her underwear.

Well, Mr Carlton, very boastie, aren't you? We shall see.

She felt less nervous now. The fear had subsided and in its stead was excitement.

At half-past three she arrived at Dyers. She decided not to

go in immediately but to walk about a little and to keep him waiting.

Ten minutes later she returned and went into the half-darkened restaurant. She looked about casually but he was not there. She heard voices from around the bar side of the place. There was an argument taking place and she recognized Carlton's voice. She looked in without entering. Carlton and another man, who was heavy-set with a bulldog face, were shouting at each other. A small crowd had gathered about them. In the middle was Dyer, the owner, who was trying to settle the dispute. He looked frightened and small.

'Now, gentlemen, please. You two grown men. No sense going on like this. You just going make trouble and cause them to shut me down.'

The Bulldog was trying to stare down Carlton. 'You feel you hard, Carlton, you feel you is a bad man, come no, gangster.'

'If is a fight you want, see me here, I not taking no back seat. You already lose at cards now you must be want lose you life.'

Mr Dyer swallowed hard and tried again to separate the two men, but he thought it prudent not to step between them.

'Croker, I'm sure Carlton wouldn't cheat you at cards. We're all gentlemen here. We know how to be civil, don't we now. Just a simple misunderstanding.'

'Is he who misunderstand if he feel he could take me for fool. I want to know how that ace reach him when I see it at the bottom of the deck? He want take me for a poppyshow? Is fifty dollars of mine he carrying in he pocket.'

'If you can't lose, don't play.'

'I bet you I broke you damn back for you, you little fucker. What the mother's you take me for anyway?'

Desmie looked on in disbelief. This was nowhere in the little scenario she had imagined. Her heart started pounding. She wanted to call out to him but she knew better than embarrass him before his friends. They were acting out their private ritual. The words would fly until there would no longer be words enough to contain the anger and then there would be violence.

The crowd became a chorus. A one foot man said to the half drunk man beside him: 'Carlton don't fraid him. I bet you they war.'

'No, man, they just a chat and fret up themselves.'

'No man, is war this time to Royal George.'

The murmuring of the crowd moved the two men along like waves of the sea. Soon they flew at each other. The Bulldog made a grab for Carlton's collar.

'You feel you is pretty. Well, you won't be pretty again.'

Dyer made a last plea which sounded like a high-pitched woman's wail.

'Please, please, all you don't mash up me place. Is just this one place me have. Go outside now.'

With that, Carlton pushed away the hand from his throat and ran outside.

Desmie screamed. Bulldog laughed.

'So you run from me, eh?'

He went out after the prey. Suddenly Carlton turned and butted him hard in his stomach and at the same time pulled the man's head down by grabbing his shirt collar and brought his own head up with all the force in his body.

Bulldog lay on the street dripping blood. He had lost two of his teeth and bitten his tongue almost off.

He was still not unconscious but sat there looking up in disbelief at what had happened to him so quickly. Then Carlton pulled out his knife.

Desmie screamed at him. 'No Carlton, please, you go kill him. You beat him already.'

Carlton heard her voice and started to come back to himself. The fury within him made him tremble. He realized that he would surely kill this man. He thought better of the knife and so merely kicked the huge hulking figure which was trying to raise itself to attack.

'You want more, come up and get it. I cut out you guts one time. You won't even self know you dead.'

Bulldog did not try to get up again.

'Another time.'

'You come near me again you is a dead man sure.'

Someone in the crowd said: 'Police coming.'

The crowd started to scatter. Carlton went back inside the bar. He ordered a drink, quite cool.

There were no charges made. Bulldog would not humiliate himself further by running to the law. It was bad enough he had lost the fight; he did not want songs written about him.

Carlton had fulfilled that day's ritual. His chorus gathered about him.

Desmie felt nauseous again. She left Dyer's quickly and returned home.

That night she relived all the incidents of the day. She

experienced the fight again and saw herself standing helplessly on the side looking on. It was foolish and disappointing. She had planned everything so carefully yet she had not seen the possibility of a stupid brawl coming between and spoiling her revelation.

Here she was, pregnant and open to the gossip of the mad vultures of the village, and the one man who could save her had no time to hear because he was too busy proving his manhood. She wanted to cry, but no tears came. No, it wasn't sadness so much she felt as anger. She was fascinated by the way he looked when he was fighting. It was hard to tell which he enjoyed more: fighting or making love.

She envied him his violence. Men seem to have all the advantages in life. They could drop their seed when they wanted. Fight when they wanted. Flee when they wanted. And what was left for her to do? Yes, she had enjoyed the love-making. She enjoyed the danger, but was it really worth it? She still did not know what he would say when he found out. All she could do was wait for the right time. But when would the right time be? Every day now she felt herself swelling.

The night spread out with all its darkness but it brought no sleep, only sounds from the yard. The stirring of animals. The scream of things pursued and captured. And then a hush.

She made up her mind. If he failed her she would hurt him. Do him some harm, possibly kill him. The decision made, dawn came on. Then she slept.

The next day she went to work. There was no morning

sickness that day, for which she was very grateful.

She went to the toilet a lot because she found herself full of liquid and yet very thirsty. Every few minutes she looked up, expecting to see Carlton entering the bank, walking with his usual swagger. But lunchtime came and he had not come.

She listened for gossip about the fight but no one said anything. She thought that strange. A big fight was always good for at least a week's circulation in town. There had been blood and the police summoned, yet there was no talk of it.

During the afternoon a figure approached her desk. She felt the presence over her like a shadow. She was so certain that it was Carlton that she did not look up and then a strange voice greeted her.

'Hello, Desmie.'

She looked up slowly to find the bespectacled figure of Gladstone Ellis peering down at her.

'Gladstone, when did you get back?'

'Last week. I asked after you and they said you were working here.'

He had a weak smile and he always held his head to one side, apologetic in manner. He had gone abroad to school. He said he would come back to teach, though few believed that anyone would be foolish enough to return to this dismal island once they had escaped. Gladstone was always reading books which caused many to distrust him. Not that he was dishonest but he must surely be mad. It was said that anyone who was too 'brainy brainy' would go mad. Only the preachers read books and then only the bible.

Gladstone was interested in politics, they had said. Maybe he would become a politician or even prime minister. There was little competition. Sometimes he wrote verse. Desmie looked up at him and past his weak smile to the time when he had slipped her a poem and walked quickly away before she could read it:

> And how shall I approach my love
> Whose stillness is like the sky above
> And how shall I take her hand
> I who am but lonely man?

She remembered the poem although she could not recall what she had done with it. Perhaps put it away with her school books. The paper would now be yellowed from time and tropical heat.

She looked at him as his lips murmured niceties. He asked about Mother Francis and whether Stephanie still lived on the island.

She wondered what would have happened had he not gone away. What if he had been the one she slept with? Could he possibly imagine what was happening inside her now? With his glasses and funny tilting head and his schoolboy poems. Would he have come by night to her grandmother's house?

He asked her to some garden party on Saturday. She said that she did not know, it depended on how she felt.

'I've not been feeling very well lately.'

'Oh well, I hope you feel better. Do try and come. . . Do you think if I came for you you might be feeling up to it?'

Foolish man, why couldn't he leave her alone and go back to his books and poems.

'Perhaps. I'll see how I feel.'

'Oh good . . . well, Saturday then.'

'I can't promise you.'

'Try.'

'Yes, all right then, I'll try.'

He walked out into the sunlight but with his leaving she felt no absence.

Saturday came and she went to the party, not that there was any real desire to go but merely a desperate attempt to keep herself from thinking. She felt herself locked up with her mind. She had to be careful. More and more she found herself thinking aloud. Perhaps she was not speaking, but she could not help feeling that her grandmother could hear her thoughts. Several times she looked up and found the old woman's eyes piercing into her.

'Is what wrong with you, girl? Why you so serious?'

'Nothing, Mother.'

'They say girls who look serious so is bad-minded.'

Mother Frances seemed relieved when Gladstone came for her. She liked Gladstone. She knew the Ellis family and was certain of the boy. She liked his listening ways. He kept such an interested expression as she went into the litany of her aches and pains.

'This boy have character,' said Mother Frances. 'You can see character on his face.'

'All I can see is his glasses,' answered Desmie.

They left for the party. Desmie could see her grandmother's face looking from the kitchen window between the carefully sewn lace curtains. Gladstone opened the door of the Ford and ushered her in. It was well cleaned for he especially wanted to impress her. She was not impressed. They owned two cars. One of which worked. He had been careful not to park in the sun, yet the car was still very hot inside. As he drove slowly along he tried to make amiable chatter. She did not help him but instead made him do all the work while she sat back with her thoughts and enjoyed the breeze which toyed with her cotton dress.

'You know Nurse Betty, don't you?' he asked.

'Not very well,' she answered, without looking at him.

A girl was taking a bath by the side of the road. She was bathing herself in a barrel which caught rainwater. She was totally unconcerned with the fact that she was visible to any passers-by.

Gladstone tried to keep his eyes forward but he could not help but turn his head to get a better view.

Desmie watched him and just to catch him said: 'You see something you like?'

He laughed uneasily. 'Just you,' he tried.

But Desmie wasn't having any. 'I'm in here, not outside.'

'Yes, I know.'

'Well, just mind that you don't run us in a ditch trying to catch a free look.'

He tried to regain his composure by adjusting his glasses.

'Don't worry, Gladstone at the controls. So tell me, what's you've been doing since I went away?'

The topic bored her. She looked from the window of the car and spoke more to the wind than to him.

'Not very much. What have you been doing? It's you who went to England.'

'Oh, just studying really.'

She wanted to say 'fool, why did you ever come back?'

'Tell me, Gladstone, don't you find this island very small compared to England?'

'Well, yes, I guess compared to England it would be very small. Geographically speaking — '

'I'm not talking geography. I mean the people.'

'Well, certainly there are more people in England. One can't expect this place to equal — '

'I mean the minds of the people, Gladstone, the minds of the people.'

'Oh, I see what you mean. Small island, small minds. Well, at least it's my island.'

She looked at him then. She couldn't help but notice the pride in his voice. He seemed to be serious. She could see him going into politics. Yes, he belonged here. But where did she belong and with whom? He did not speak again until they reached the party. She was grateful.

Nurse Betty Riley lived in a well cared for house which was left to her by her mother. Desmie had known her as a schoolgirl but they were never really close. Betty became a nurse which made her even more remote from Desmie.

Nursing was a good occupation for a girl who came from the country. But it was a step down from what Mother Frances would have wanted for her granddaughter. It was one thing to marry a doctor and quite another to be a nurse. A nurse came in contact with too many naked men. She was always suspect. One could tell from the fact that her eyes did not betray timidity but instead seemed too aware.

There was a lively crowd present. Music was playing on the gramophone and several couples were dancing. The kitchen was the centre of activity, filled with smells of ham and chicken. Nurse Betty moved in and out between the different circles of guests making sure the men had plenty to eat and drink. Desmie did not have to be introduced; everyone knew her. Nurse Betty gave her a big gold-toothed smile and watched her from behind her eyes. Desmie looked at her and thought of what her teacher had told her so long ago.

'A lady of class should wear gold on her fingers, wrist or neck. Never in her mouth or about her ankles.'

Desmie did not like to think of herself as snobbish or putting on airs, but she could not help the fact that she was not common.

She sipped lemonade and let herself be danced with by Gladstone and two others who asked her. When a fourth asked her she refused politely, saying she needed to rest a while. After all, she did not know him and he seemed to be sweating from too much strong drink.

She walked about the house in search of the bathroom. She noticed that Betty kept the place very clean. The furniture was not the best but everything was tidy. On the wall was an old wedding picture of the mother, who looked tiny and Victorian, beside a tall and awkward-looking man whose hair was parted in the middle. The eyes of the woman seemed sad as only West Indian women can be. Desmie looked at the photograph for a long while and tried to understand why the expression on the face seemed so familiar to her. It was a look not so much of resignation as it was of waiting.

Desmie turned to find Betty standing and watching her. 'Oh girl, I was just looking at this photograph. Is that your mother?'

'Yes. You like it?'

'It's a beautiful wedding dress.'

'Why don't you come join the party. You not eating or drinking anything.'

'Oh, I'm having some lemonade.'

'But you not hungry, girl? Have some food no.'

'Not just now, maybe later.'

She could not explain that she never would eat outside unless she knew the person for years and years. Too many years of Mother Frances drumming into her tales of obeah and poisoning at the hands of jealous people. She could hear her grandmother saying: 'Once they put that poison in you, you can't get it out you know. You just waste away until you dead like stone.'

Suddenly Desmie felt foolish. How much control did she have over her. How distant she had made her from everyone else. She would have loved to be able to beg Betty for advice. She was a nurse, she could tell her what to take to stop this baby which would ruin her life. Nurses knew things. It was an everyday business. They knew what to do and what to take. Maybe it would have been better if she had become a nurse. But what would Mother Frances say? What difference what she said? Could it be any worse than what she would do if she knew that her only granddaughter was pregnant? Suddenly Desmie realized that Betty was speaking to her.

'Desmie, are you all right?'

'Oh yes, fine.'

'I'm glad my cousin bring you.'

'Your cousin?'

'Gladstone. Is me cousin, he never tell you?'

'No — well, I guess there's no reason why he should. Well, that's that.'

'Pardon?' Betty looked at her strangely.

'Nothing. I think I'll have some of that chicken after all. It smell so good.'

Betty went off to get her a plate.

That would have been something, Desmie thought. What if I had asked her for help? She would have run and told him. By tomorrow even the dead would know I was pregnant.

Betty brought her a plate of chicken and rice. She ate little and still felt nauseous.

They left the party early while new guests were just arriving. The party was just beginning to take on a new rhythm of its own. The sound of the gramophone gave off more defiant sounds as Betty played the special records which she held in reserve. The laughter was mixed with the sounds of car doors slamming as the new figures emerged. By midnight the party would really be in full swing. The dancing, sweating bodies would be more insistent. The voices less coherent. It was a weekend, so the celebrants could fete without guilt. But Desmie did not stay for the climax. Gladstone left reluctantly but politely, to escort her home. On the ride home he asked if she felt any better. This only served to annoy her more. She answered sharply, 'Fine, just fine.'

'Is something the matter, Desmie?'

'The matter? Nothing's the matter. I just have an, upset stomach, that's all.'

'Well, you'll be home soon.'

He paused and took in the clear night sky with the full moon.

'You know that if you ever needed anything you could count on me.'

'Beg pardon?'

'I said that if you ever needed anything you could depend on me.'

She looked at him with suspicion.

'What could I need?'

She felt like being really malicious and adding 'what *you* could give me?' but she didn't.

'Well, just remember, I'll be there.'

'Yes, well, thank you, Gladstone, goodnight. You better go back to the party.'

He took his leave of her very slowly. Stopping to watch her enter the door of the house. She did not know what it was about him that she found so annoying. It seemed that the more solicitous he became the more disgusting she found him. He was foolish the way a mosquito was foolish. Buzzing about your ear. Perhaps it was because there was nothing really dangerous about the man. He was just an innocuous discomfort.

As she closed the door behind her and rested against it, she said aloud: 'The mosquito.'

She listened for the sound of his car pulling away. Finally it came. Even that was a small sound.

Mother Frances called from upstairs. 'Desmie, is that you?'

'Yes, Mother, it's me.'

She thought to herself: 'Oh God, that's all I need, she's still up.'

'You home early.'

'It's not so early.'

She heard the sound of her grandmother's slippers coming down the steps.

'Didn't you have a good time?'

'Fine, why?'

'You don't usually come home before midnight. What's the matter?'

'I just felt tired, Mother, I don't really know those people anyway.'

Mother Frances started to heat up some milk, and then she sat herself down beside the table in the kitchen.

Desmie didn't feel up to more discussion so she began to make her way towards the stairs. Lately she had found the best method for avoiding argument was to retreat whenever Mother Frances entered the room.

'Going to bed, dear?'

'Yes, Mother, feel kind of tired.'

'You know, Desmie, that Gladstone is a nice boy.'

'Yes, very nice boy, Mother, goodnight.'

'What you make up your mind for do?'

'What do you mean make my mind for do?'

Mother Frances looked surprised at the response.

'You don't have to jump down me throat-hole every time me ask you little something, you know.'

'I'm not jumping — I just don't understand what you mean.'

'Well, I can't live too much longer. You over eighteen, I feel you should be thinking of giving me some grandchildren before me dead.'

Desmie felt herself wanting to explode. She wanted to vomit there in front of her. Maybe expose herself. Instead she went up the stairs and, half lifting her head, said; 'Goodnight, Mother.'

It was Monday morning when she finally made a decision.

She had wondered why she had heard no news of Carlton. He had not tried to reach her. No one spoke of his whereabouts. Desmie weighed everything in her mind and came to the conclusion that something must be very wrong. The only possible reason why he had not come to her must be that he was in danger, possibly injured or dead. In fact, after two sleepless nights Desmie decided that the only pardonable excuse was an almost fatal accident. If he was not violently hurt then she would surely see to it that he would be.

She went at lunch to the taxi-cab stand where she knew Carlton's feisty friend waited for passengers. As she saw him she tried not to make it apparent that it was he she sought but the certainty of his laughter made it obvious that he knew. As she entered his cab she asked to be driven to Dyers. Along the way she allowed him to prattle on as he beat the side of the cab to a calypso record on the radio. When they reached the cafe she went to pay him his money and used the opportunity to ask: 'By the way, you haven't seen Carlton, have you?'

He grinned a big gap-toothed grin and said, 'You know, I say to meself, I bet you she go ask for Carlton.'

'Well, have you seen him or haven't you? I thought perhaps he was — '

'Oh, he's all right. He just go way for a week until things come quiet again. You know somebody try and give him some chat, and well, you know Softcandle not a man to back down. Anyhow, he soon come.'

Desmie thanked him and walked away towards the restaurant. Well, at least he wasn't arrested. She would have preferred to hear that he was injured. Not near death, but slightly wounded. At least that would excuse his not contacting her.

She consoled herself. It's understandable that he had to go into hiding.

It was Wednesday night. The nights seemed to be becoming longer and more airless. It was not just in her mind. It had not rained for two weeks, which was very strange on the island. Usually it rained for at least an hour every day. The rain caused the intense greenness of the island's foliage which was sometimes painfully beautiful to the eye. Now there was no rain and the old people were murmuring about drought. The farmers would bend close to the earth like trees and whisper their fears.

Desmie kept stirring in bed trying to will herself to sleep, but only succeeded in making herself perspire more. She could hear the old woman snoring in the next room. Suddenly she heard the dog barking in the yard. She had a feeling that someone was there but did not move from her.

Desmie kept stirring in bed trying to will herself to sleep, but only succeeded in making herself perspire more. She could hear the old woman snoring in the next room. Suddenly she heard the dog barking in the yard. She had a feeling that someone was there but did not move from her bed. She followed the barking sound with her eyes from the bed. The dog ran to one side of the house and then to the other. The snoring stopped. She heard Mother Frances wake. The heavy creaking of the bed next door and her grandmother's voice.

'But what wrong with that dog at all?'

The sound of slippered feet pacing.

'Desmie, is you that?'

'No, Mother.'

'Is what do that dog? Is like he seeing duppy.'

'Must be the heat, Mother.'

'Shut up dog and let people sleep. I bet you I poison you.'

The dog kept up a steady barking. The two women waited for the sounds of growling and combat which would mean that he found whatever it was which was disturbing him. No growls came.

'I wonder if somebody out there trying for tief?'

Then the barking stopped.

'Well, he stop now. Dog must be mad.'

'Is the heat, Mother, go back to bed.'

The old woman went back to bed and Desmie lay on her bed staring at the clearing darkness and grateful for the coming dawn.

Thursday afternoon Carlton met her after work. She expected him. He was behind her but she knew him without turning.

He smiled and touched his hat in greeting. Half arrogance, half boyish charm.

'I hear you was asking for me.'

'I only ask if you were all right.'

'So you didn't want to see me?'

She started walking and he followed alongside trying to look casual.

'Why should I want to see you, you don't want to see me, do you?'

'Of course I want to see you. I'm sorry for what happen last time but I didn't really have a choice.'

'You could have written.'

'Yes, well, I figured I better wait until I see you to explain in person, you know what I mean. I don't let people walk over me, you understand. That fellow — '

'I don't really want to know.'

They walked along in silence for a while. He watched three small boys pitching pennies against a wall. She wondered if he were seeing himself.

'So, you miss me?' he asked, turning towards her with a grin and then looking away.

'No.'

'You lie.'

'You like yourself, don't you?'

'So what was it you had to tell me?'

'It's nothing. Not important.'

He could see from her eyes that she wanted him to ask again.

'What was it?'

'It doesn't matter, I said.'

'You want to go to Dyers?'

'No, not there again.'

They walked on until they came by the sea wall. They watched as the waves struck and receded. White foam full of secrets and history. The strong salt smell of the sea always frightened her. There was power there which always made her feel naked and frightened.

After they stood for some time in one spot, they suddenly started walking again. Though neither of them spoke, they felt the change of mood together the same instant.

As they walked they passed two boys walking along the footpath. Desmie noted that one of the boys wore heavy combat boots which looked several sizes too large for him. The boy wore no socks and the shoes kept slipping as he made striding, military-like steps. The boy did not mind the inconvenience because at least the shoes protected him from the burning heat of the rocky road. The other boy wore trousers which were worn so badly in the seat that his backside was half exposed. He himself seemed to take no notice of this; he laughed at the way Desmie tried to turn her head away from the sight.

Carlton looked at her and smiled. 'Poor people here like to shame you with they misery. Is like they use it as a weapon.'

She never felt guilty about the poverty of others. Her grandmother had given her good training in dealing with servants. She knew how to speak in a low but clear voice which would communicate not only commands but respect. She had learned since childhood that she was of a very special family and that although she must be kind to the majority she must never become like them.

They walked on and watched the sudden movement of clouds in the sky. It was not the clouds so much that gave the warning. It was the quick and desperate lashing of the sea.

'Weather changing,' said Carlton, and they began to move back towards the town.

Soon the raindrops started falling. A strange and rhythmic falling which the trees began whispering about.

They ran on to the taxi stand and Carlton covered her with his jacket. Soon they were inside the taxi and moving up the long road towards his house. She did not ask him where he was taking her. She accepted it, as she did the falling of the rain. How good the island looked now and how strange the way the rain came without warning. Every day the farmers were waiting and every night they too slept in the stifling heat, waiting like Desmie, waiting.

The house looked larger somehow. The bedroom smelled of cigarette smoke and liquor. Carlton opened the shutters to let the air in.

'Do you mind the rain?'

The thunder frightened her and the lightning, but it was all right there inside the house with him.

He undressed her quickly without asking her. He dried her carefully with a towel as though she were a child and he the father. She made sure to stare directly into his eyes so that he could see that she was not turning away from him. Almost as if she was daring him.

First he made long slow careful moves inside her and then short quick ones. It seemed a long time since they had made love.

The wind was shaking the shutters. That made her hold him tightly. She was totally free now. She had no fears of becoming pregnant because she was already on the other side of danger. She wanted him to be gentle at first. Now she wanted him to be rough, very rough. She had heard somewhere that sometimes when men made love to a pregnant woman it made the baby drop. She wanted him to make love to her over and over again. As long as the rain lasted. Maybe it would be a hurricane and destroy everything. Destroy the whole island with all its gossiping eyes and voices. Wreck the bank where she worked. Smash down the church. Crush her house and the yard. Perhaps the sea would come up and wash away the dead.

Wash away the whole town. It would be all right to die now, like this, in bed with Carlton. No one would ever know and if they did, what would it matter? Just two more entwined bodies among the rubble. Who could tell that she was with child? What would two bodies matter among so many? What better way to die? She had no desire to grow old like Mother Frances. No desire to be like the old and overdressed women who seemed to keep going out of spite. If there was a God, why did he seem to take everything away at the wrong time?

Those who wanted to die, lived. Those who wanted to live —

She heard herself screaming. He was doing something inside her. Moving from side to side between her where her wanting was.

'Oh God, Carlton, don't stop, please don't stop now.'

And what would happen to the birds? Where were they hiding now? She couldn't hear them. Only the lashing of the rain and wind through the trees. And the lightning flashing like once when she saw a tree set afire and it terrified her to know that God could do that from heaven so far away. And Mother Frances had said that his wrath could strike down the wicked the same way. With bolts of lightning which would find you no matter where you tried to hide.

'But who are the wicked, Mother?'

'God knows who they are.'

'But do the wicked know that they are wicked?'

'They know when they are doing wickedness.'

'How do they know?'

'They know because they feel it.'

Then wickedness must be that thing that feels so good that you know that you shouldn't be doing it. Like that thing which Carlton was doing inside her now. Inside of her darkness.

She had not meant to cry. She did not like to cry before him. It was something that came on her without warning. She sent him from the room to get her some water. She stood up and pulled the sheet around her, and collected herself before he returned.

The room smelled of lovemaking. The bed was sticky from their bodies. She smelled the salt water from the sea. It had gotten into the bed and into their bodies. She was not ashamed of the it. He had a good smell: not like the goat odour of the men in the village, the men who worked the roads or planted and cut cane. It was a good smell, the unmistakable smell of orgasm. But now she wanted to bathe and be clean when she told him what she had to.

She washed alone. He wanted to bathe with her but she said no. She came out and dressed. The rain was dying. He smoked a cigarette he seemed to enjoy.

'Carlton, I'm pregnant.'

'You what?' He put the cigarette to rest in the ashtray, which was full.

'Why don't you empty the ashtray.'

He got up and started to empty the ashtray as though given a command. He was glad of the diversion.

'I said I'm pregnant.'

'You sure?'

'Yes, I'm sure. I didn't want to be sure, but I'm sure.'

He paused a while. This was very sudden. He had noticed something different in her lovemaking. Something more desperate, more open.

'Well, I'll take care of the child, so don't worry.'

He had said this many times before. She could tell by his tone. He had made many young country girls pregnant, and had made many visits to their homes by night. He would bring a chicken or two, possibly buy them a dress or shoes. He would leave ten or twenty dollars behind on the table in the morning when he'd depart. They would be glad for the sight of him. He would see them all at least once a month, maybe twice if they were exceptional.

'I don't want you to care for the child.'

'Oh no?' What was it she wanted then? It didn't matter. She was worth whatever it would cost him. She was class. A prize possession. They would all envy him in the town when they knew. He had finally broken her. Finally gotten past her wall. That aloofness which he could not seem to conquer even with sex.

'You want me marry you; is all right, don't fret. I'll marry you, yes.'

She suddenly started to laugh. At first he joined in with her, thinking that he had ended her fear, but then he noticed the mockery in her laughter and began to grow angry.

'Is why you laugh? You think is lie me lie? I say I go marry you.'

She stopped laughing and looked directly at him.

'And who tell you I want to marry?'

'How you mean? All girls want for marry.' He looked incredulous.

She spoke very calm and low: 'Yes, every girl might want to marry, but not to you, Carlton.'

He jumped to his feet and circled about her. 'And what's wrong with me? Plenty girls begging me for marry them. Is what you come here for?'

She could see that he was hurt. She knew that he was most dangerous when hurt. He had the same look which she saw in his eyes when he had pulled the knife on the fellow in the street. It frightened her but she liked it because it was electric and dangerous. She realized that she had made him feel small and that she would have to be careful in withdrawing herself from his anger.

He lit a cigarette again.

'Is because you gone school you feel you better than me. Well, let me tell you, I never go school but I can make do without it. I could survive anywhere.'

'I'm sure you could, Carlton.'

'Well, don't make sport of me because I don't have schooling.'

She could smell the scent of mangoes which had fallen outside in the heavy rain. It was a warm and hungry smell. Then came the mixed scent of cinnamon and orange blossom. The earth had opened up. The rain had filled where the thirst was. She looked at Carlton and tried to still his raging.

'I'm not making sport of you, Carlton. Yes, I went to school. I never really liked it, but I went. The seat used to feel hot there in their classroom. I always wanted to go make number one and Teacher Biddy would make me sit and wait. It was no great thing going to school.'

His face remained tense. He could not really deal with these girls who came from large houses with stairs and antique furniture. He could not really control them the way he could the village girls who had one dress and one panty.

'It's not schooling, so then what it is why you won't marry me?'

'It's not that easy, Carlton.'

'Why? Because of you grandmother? Why you don't just run way and leave her?'

Desmie looked up at the triangular construction of the ceiling. She wondered if he had built it.

'Did you build this house, Carlton?'

He looked up at the ceiling where her eyes had strayed.

'I helped build it, yes, but don't bother worry bout the ceiling. It's marriage I asking about.'

She knew he would not be put off. 'All right, you want to know why I won't marry you?'

'Yes, it's your grandmother and you people.'

'It's not just her. It's because I couldn't stand to see you going out every night to your different women and your gambling and all the rest of it.'

He laughed. This he could understand.

'Well, you know I would always come home.'

'That's not really good enough.'

'Well, a man must go out. He can't just stay lock up.'

'I don't really think I'm for marriage, Carlton.'

For an instant she saw herself in one of the small airless shacks which the country girls used for homes. She saw herself gossiping over a fence at dawn like the other women, or waiting beside a road with nothing in her eyes but boredom and hatred for the man who had conquered her youth.

'Well, what is it you want girl? You say you pregnant. What you go do? Is somebody else you pregnant for?'

She saw that he felt awkward.

'I won't even answer that. Do you think I would be here with you if there was somebody else I was pregnant for?'

'No, I don't feel you're like that. Well then, what you want do?'

She got up and walked to the window and looked out into the still damp evening.

'They say there are things you can do if you don't wait too late.'

He walked over beside her. 'You would do that?'

'I don't have too much choice, do I? I don't really want to. Is there a doctor you could trust?'

He thought for a moment.

'No one here on this island. If we could go away for a while I could get someone.'

'Go way? How I could do that?'

'You could tell her that you want to go on holiday with you girlfriends.'

The thought had crossed her mind before. Would it work this time?

'It would be hard. I think she already suspects something.'

He touched her hair and moved her towards him easily.

'And afterwards there would be no need to come back here.'

She laughed. 'Just stay with you.'

'Why not? I'll look after you.'

'And what happen when you get tired of me?'

'I would never get tired of you.'

A small lizard climbed the wall out of the damp.

'Oh no. You say you would never get tired, but if you did —'

'I wouldn't.'

'I would never be able to come home again, would I?'

He began to stroke her body in an effort to knead away her fear.

'Take a chance, girl, take a chance.'

While outside the fireflies flew and shone bright.

The next day she began to tackle Mother Frances. She knew that it would not be easy. The pain of the disaster of the attempted Christmas escape was still fresh in her mind. She would have to be careful not to over-anticipate. Not to give any sign of just how important this trip was to her. At the same time she could not afford too much waiting. Each day made the prospect of abortion more and more dangerous. She would have to enlist Stephanie again. It was already too late to worry about caution. Stephanie knew that she was pregnant and if she were going to tell then she would have already done so. In any case, it would be impossible to manage this escape without her.

Desmie tried to make herself plan everything in a slow, deliberate and dispassionate manner. As if it were someone else whom she was giving advice to. She wrote it all in a small notebook: You must take out three hundred dollars from your savings. Carlton says that he will get money but nothing is ever certain with him. You must take a good amount of clothes but not too much to make Mother Francis suspicious. Any more suspicious than she already is. Carlton says that he knows of a doctor who will perform the operation. It might be that he really doesn't know anyone. If I can't have it done safely then I won't do it at all. If I cannot get rid of the child then I will never come back here.

I must not be afraid.

Lord, I am afraid. If you do not help me I will curse you always.

The next day she began to put her plan into operation. First she got in touch with Stephanie. She told her about the idea of travelling to Barbados for the operation. Stephanie didn't reply for a long while but gave a wicked smile. Her eyes sparkled like a firefly. Then she said, 'All right then.'

The plan was for Stephanie to come and ask Desmie's grandmother to let her go with her. There would be more chance of Mother Frances saying yes then. Stephanie came for dinner the following night. She was full of girlish charm and chatter. Stephanie complimented the old woman on her beautiful garden with all the beautiful spices and scents. Mother Frances seemed won over. She smiled like a schoolgirl. Over the meal Stephanie made mention of the trip.

'It would be so nice if Dee could come. We would have so much fun, and I would look after her.'

The old woman smiled knowingly. 'And who would take care of you, girl?'

'Well, we could take care of each other.'

'And what about her job?'

Desmie spoke up quickly, perhaps too quickly. 'Oh, I could take a holiday.'

Mother Frances sighed. 'Well, I don't know, I not feeling too well these days. Is like me have one foot there in the grave.'

'But Mother, you were saying how much better you feeling since Christmas.'

The old woman looked at her with eyes wide. 'When me say so?'

'Just last Sunday, Mother.'

'Well it comes and goes.'

Stephanie pursed her lips and touched them softly with a napkin to reveal a cat's smile.

'Well, Mother Frances, you wouldn't stop Desmie from having a holiday, would you?'

'Desmie all right, she have she whole life for holiday. I gone soon.'

By the end of the meal little had been gained. The old woman was not easy. Often she would keep quiet and then just when they thought that she might be submitting she would suddenly say, as if speaking to herself, 'I don't think so, you know.'

'But why not, Mother Frances?'

'I don't think the time right just now.'

'But when will be the right time?'

'What's the rush anyway? Too eager make sorry.'

The meal died slowly.

Afterwards the girls whispered together in the corner.

'Well,' Stephanie said, 'if she don't let you go then you just have to run away.'

The words fell heavily on Desmie. She had thought of this but was in dread of such a decision. She preferred to hope that the old woman could be moved. There was always hope but she would have to be careful not to seem to want it too much. Any time Mother Frances saw that she wanted anything too much, she always refused her.

As Stephanie was leaving she kissed Mother Frances goodbye and then, turning to Desmie, whispered, 'Why don't you kill her?'

In the twilight her eyes looked like a lizard's. How easily she had said it. The thought frightened Desmie. Stephanie was a girl completely without conscience. But this was not what frightened Desmie. It was the fact that she too had thought of it many times in the quiet of her room. Sometimes before falling asleep. Sometimes in her dreams. She had thought of some way doing it. It was never any clear plan like poison or pushing her down a flight of stairs. It was something vague but persistent. Kill this old woman before she kills you.

That night she wrote in her notebook: I will try.

Mother Frances went to bed at her usual time of nine o'clock. She would start to doze about eight thirty and then move herself upstairs to read her bible for ten minutes or so, which, with the 'begats', never failed to bring her to gentle sleep.

Desmie stayed up and paced about downstairs listening to the crickets and the other conspiratorial sounds of the night. She began to feel foolish. She had brought Stephanie around to the house to beg for her; it had all proved quite useless. Mother Frances seemed to know just what she was doing. Time was against her. She could no longer try to win her way with guile: she would have to be more direct.

The next morning, when Mother Frances woke her to get ready for work, she kept to her bed.

'What wrong, Desmie, you no hear me call three times already? Me never see a girl love she bed so.'

Desmie turned her head back towards the wall.

'I'm not going to work today.'

'Why you not going, something wrong with you?'

'Yes, I need a holiday.'

'Oh, so you is a holiday you need. And what I must tell you people them at the bank?'

'Tell them I'm not coming in.'

Mother Frances took a long pause to fully understand the situation.

'Oh, I see. Stephanie is a very pretty girl.'

Desmie turned to look at her grandmother. What was she on about now?

'What?'

'Me say Stephanie is a very pretty girl. She pretty like pretty self.'

'And so?'

'Well, must be she tell you for try this.'

'She never tell me anything.'

'Oh yes, well mek me tell you something. I not born yesterday so don't take me make no poppyshow. I say you not going Barbados with she and that's final. So if you want lay in you bed you lay there. You not going out of my sight. That young girl there too brazen and she eye them too damn bright. Me mind tell me — '

'Your mind always telling you something.'

'Me mind tell me something not right.'

With this Mother Frances walked from the room. Desmie felt the nausea come on her again. She got up quickly and grabbed the pot from beneath her bed. She threw up so violently that the room started to spin. Her grandmother heard her from downstairs and came back up to see what was the matter.

'Desmie, is you that? Why you throwing up so? I feel you need a dose of salts for purge you. Twice last week I hear you.'

Desmie sat down on the bed and tried to control her heavy breathing. The room stank of vomit. The walls seemed to be closing in tighter now. The only thought in her mind was that she must get this woman away from her. Better to go to work than to stay home. She couldn't tell how long she could control herself.

'Is a good purge you need, girl.'

'I don't need any purge, Mother.'

'Then what wrong with you then?'

'Nothing wrong with me.'

'What kind of nothing that make you vomit so every minute?'

Desmie turned her face away from her and reached for her housecoat. She slipped it quickly over the chemise she wore. But already she could feel the dark eyes of the old woman boring into her. She must get out of this room now. But it was too late. Mother Francis grabbed her with her thin strong hands. The arms filled with veins and the silver bracelets she wore clanged together.

'Desmie, I talking to you, girl, don't twist way from me. Me ask you what wrong?'

She ran from the room and down the stairs, but where could she go? The house was not hers. The garden was not hers. The island was hers.

She found herself down the stairs although she could not remember walking down them. She heard her grandmother's voice calling after her. Coming down at her, forcing her against the wall. The first thing that came to her mind was to fasten her housecoat about her. She did not want her to see the swelling of her body.

'Me ask you what wrong with you?'

'Nothing, I said. Nothing wrong with me. Why you can't leave me alone?'

She thought of going to the bathhouse to bathe but suddenly she was more frightened to be caught naked. Perhaps there would be lizards in there. She hated stepping on lizards, especially barefoot. Something in her mind flashed back to Stephanie. Perhaps it was because Stephanie had the eyes of a lizard. She heard the old woman coming down the steps.

'Why don't you go and bathe?'

'I don't — I don't want to bathe now.'

She felt the slyness in the old woman's voice. She meant to trip her. She was spinning a web all about her.

She could smell the pungent odour of lye and disinfectant coming from outside. The old woman must be making soap again, she thought. She hated the fumes. Once a month Mother Frances would make her own soap to wash her clothes. Sometimes she would give some to the neighbours. Now especially the fumes made her nauseous. She thought: Oh God, please don't make me vomit again.

'Is why you fraid for take physic?'

'I just don't want it, that's all.'

'You acting peculiar, you know. Me feel is something you want hide.'

Desmie opened the door and went out the front of the house.

'Is where you going, girl? You better put on some clothes.'

Desmie started to sit down on the porch of the house. She looked down and saw a lizard close to her foot. It gave her a scare. She jumped up and then heard the laughter of Perkins who was outside working on the garden.

'Morning, Missy, seem like lizard frighten you.'

Desmie didn't answer him. She despised his mocking tone. She went back inside the house to her grandmother's stare. She decided to go back to bed. She was safest there. She took an orange from the table and started to climb the stairs, looking back over her shoulder at the old woman as she did so. Just as she reached the top she heard Mother

Frances say: 'I think I better send for Dr Edwards.'

The words struck the girl like a fist.

'No, don't send for him.'

'I go send for him yes, something not right.'

Then the old woman opened the door and called out: 'Perkins!'

'Yes, M'am?'

'Go into town and call Dr Edwards for me. Tell him me say come.'

'Yes, M'am.'

'Go now, Perkins, don't stop on the way. Tell he Miss Desmie sick.'

The girl felt her heart pounding. She ran down the stairs to say something, but when she reached the bottom she could find no words. The tears fell. She heard the motor of the car start up and saw Perkins from the window give a glance towards the house as he drove off. There was mockery in that glance. She felt he knew everything.

The old woman must also know. They were all playing with her like spiders, like lizards. She turned to look at her grandmother and saw the way she had her head cocked to one side and held her right wrist by her left hand. It was a gesture one used before an inevitable triumph. Her head started to spin. Her mouth felt dry and she had to strain to make some words. But even as she did so it did not sound like her voice.

'Mother, I don't want to see any doctor.'

'Well, you could want or don't want, he coming now.'

She climbed the stairs slowly again and entered her room to await the end.

It was some time before Dr Edwards came. In the interim fear had given place to acceptance. She no longer cared. She was glad to be free of struggle. For the first hour she had thought of dressing and running from the house but she soon realized that it would make no difference. She would be found out anyway. Perhaps she could talk to Dr Edwards alone and persuade him not to tell. Maybe he might not know himself that she was pregnant.

Dr Edwards was close to sixty. He had thick wire glasses that fitted uneasily around his face. They magnified his sad eyes and serious face, and he seemed to be able to see right through you. Desmie soon realized it was useless to try and fool him.

The old woman did not want to leave the room during the examination. Desmie finally begged him: 'Dr Edwards, please make her leave.'

This request only served to make Mother Frances all the more suspicious.

'She up to some wickedness.'

She kept vigil outside the closed door of the room.

The doctor touched Desmie's stomach and looked at her swollen breasts and then removed his glasses. She felt the need to say something quickly before he did.

'Doctor, I don't understand what happened but — '

'What don't you understand?'

'Well, I've been feeling sort of — '

'Pregnant,' he whispered.

The blood pounded in her head.

'But I don't know how. . .'

'There's only one way unless you're the Virgin Mary.'

'Oh God, Dr Edwards, what am I going to do? I want to die.'

'No Desmie, you're not going to die. It happens every day. Every hour of every day in fact. It's just life.'

'But my grandmother — '

'I'll talk to her. Meanwhile you just rest for a while.'

He rubbed her forehead gently and felt the pounding along her temples. His hand seemed to soothe her. He gave her some pills to make her sleep. He only gave her two. She would have liked to have taken the whole bottle. She felt herself falling into a nice darkness. The voices inside her head became silent. When he was certain she had fallen asleep he went outside to the still-waiting woman.

She fell inside a dream. The fumes of the homemade soap still invaded her, even in her sleep. There was colour too. A green like the vegetation of the island. She was walking through a field. Someone was with her. It must have been Carlton although she could not make out his face. She felt the strength of his hands leading her, then she noticed the peculiar feminine thinness of his wrist.

They went into his house and she remembered the blue paint of his bedroom and the stucco walls. She lay down on his bed and tried to pull him down with her, but he was saying something. He said that the old people were watching them. She looked to see who was watching but only saw the huge mango tree which faced his window. Were they up in the mango tree, Carlton? She remembered that she should cover her body so she was trying to pull the sheets over them to hide them from view. But now something was striking at the soles of her feet.

'Wake up, girl, you want kill me?'

Desmie opened her eyes and tried to remember where she was. The pill had made her very weak. Then, in a flash, she realized where she was and what was happening. Mother Frances was pulling the bedclothes from her in a frenzy.

'You want kill me with shame? How could you do it, girl? Everything I work so hard for.'

'I didn't — '

'Don't lie. If you lie to me any more I strike you dead. Doctor tell me you making baby. I know something wasn't right. I could feel it. Is who you breeding for? Is that worthless gambler boy you bring here, ain't it?'

'Mother!'

'Answer me. Is that damn nasty boy Carlton. So that is why you want go Barbados.'

'I'm sorry.'

Desmie sat up in the bed and tried to cover herself.

'You sorry? You not sorry yet, girl. Take off them clothes.'

With that, the old woman ripped the chemise from her.

'Go on, beat me. Beat me if you want to.'

The woman slapped her until she grew weary, then she ran to the window and started to scream.

'Oh God, oh God, why you let me live to see this shame? Why you punish me so, Lord? Why you didn't let me just dead?.

'Mother, I didn't want this to happen.'

'You didn't want it to happen, then why you sleep with this wicked neaga man so? All you schooling, all I try and try and now see what happen. Oh God, I go dead. Girl, you not shame?'

'Yes, mother, I shame.'

'Is who tell you to do it? It must be that piss-and-tail

girlfriend of yours. She grow up too fast.'

'Nobody tell me to do it.'

'Well, is force he force you?'

'No, Mother.'

'If he rape you then I see to it that he never trouble a next girl. I make sure they chop off his privates. Tell me if he force you?'

She shook the girl until the bed started to tremble.

'No, Mother, he never force me.'

'He no force you. Well, then, get out. Get out, I say. I swear me don't want see you again.'

She dragged the girl naked from the bed and pulled her to the steps.

'No, Mother, please.'

Just then the woman looked up and saw the leering grin of Perkins.

'Mistress Frances, you call me?'

'I ain't call you. What you want in here?'

'I thought you did call me.'

'Me say me never call you. Get out.'

'Yes, M'am.'

Perkins made a slow retreat as Desmie ran back into her room and covered herself. Her heart was pounding. Why had the doctor left her alone with her, Mother Frances? He said he would make her understand. Could anyone be trusted? They said things to you. They rubbed your head and gave you soothing words and then they left you to die alone.

Seeing the mockery on Perkins' face pulled the old woman out of her hysteria. She realized that the girl had to be protected now from gossiping people like this. She came back into the room.

Desmie sat crying in the corner close to the wall. Her only thoughts were that she made less of an adversary from a sitting position. Perhaps the old woman would not be so angry if she did not stand up to oppose her. Through her tears she could see her sit down on the bed. She seemed lost in thought. The girl continued to cry.

'Stop it. Stop you bawling.'

Desmie did not listen to her.

'Stop you bawling, I said. It's too late for that now. You want me to lock you outside?'

'No.'

'Well, then, stop it. We have to decide what to do.'

'He says — '

'He says what?'

'He says . . . that he loves me.'

The old woman looked at her and sucked her teeth.

'Cho, what he know about love? All him know is for drop the seed when he ready. Now you belly get big he won't have no more time for you. The village is full of young chupid girl who hot tween they legs. What he need you for now?'

Now Desmie stopped crying. She felt insulted.

'He say he marry me.'

'Marry you and then what?'

It was true. The same thought had entered her mind. She had not wanted to marry this man.

'You mother dead in America working for you. I promised her I would look after you. All her hopes and dreams were for you, and now what? Girl, you think that all we work for so hard in my life we going leave it to some worthless drunken neaga man like Carlton? Not me. I rather you have a bastard child than to see you marry he. I swear to God I choke you to death myself before I see you marry to him. God forgive me and pardon me for saying so.' The old woman crossed herself.

Her eyes suddenly grew big as if she had seen a jumbie. She jumped up and grabbed hold of her daughter by the wrist.

'Come, kneel down and pray with me.'

The girl was frightened. She did not know what to do. She felt violated. It would have been better if the woman had just beaten her.

'I say kneel down and ask God to forgive you or I swear I kick you out this Jesus morning.'

Desmie got on her knees and prayed. She did not know what to say. No words came to her but the tears fell again and her knees felt sore against the harsh straw mat at the side of the bed. She looked down and concentrated on the circular patterns of the mat and she felt herself becoming dizzy.

'Where you bible, girl?'

'It's there, on the dresser.'

The old woman grabbed the bible and forced it into the girl's hand.

'Swear to me that you will follow what I tell you.'

'I swear, Mother.'

'Swear that you will obey and do just what I tell you. You will never sleep with this man again.'

'I swear.'

'Swear on your unborn child.'

The woman took the girl's hand and put it on her swollen belly.

'Swear!'

'I swear.'

'All right. I won't throw you out but you must do exactly

what I tell you. From this day you not walking back into town until you baby born. I don't want anybody to see your shame. I am going to make certain of that. I'll see to it that no harm come to you but after the baby born I'm shipping you out of here. From this day forward I never going trust you again.'

With that, the woman got up and took the bible from the girl's hand and spat on the ground before her.

And so began the second phase of the rising.

THE STILLNESS

Mother Frances began on a new campaign now. It was she who employed silence. Hardly a word passed between her and Desmie. The morning stretched itself lazily into afternoon. Meals were given in silence. Objects pointed to or indicated by a movement of the head. It was as if the old woman hoped to force her granddaughter into repentance by isolation.

At first the girl was glad for the stillness. There was little to be said anyway. All that was left was to await the inevitable. She watched herself getting heavier daily and more full of sleep. The heat conspired against her and made walking more difficult. She had never really liked walking anyway. She preferred to be driven. But slowly the lack of choice began to irritate her. She was forced to give up her job. The threat became reality. She was not allowed out of the house for any length of time. She soon realized that this was to be solitary confinement. At least there were no more sickening lectures. When the seed has already been planted there is nothing to do but await its harvest so that the rotten fruit can be plucked out. That was the way of it.

There were times when the silence became deafening. The

old woman seated at table would look through the girl, or sometimes stare at the girl's spirit which was the third person seated at table.

Friends came to visit in the beginning. They were made to feel uncomfortable. They soon stopped coming.

The only outings were the Sunday church services. Only then did Mother Frances bother to speak to her.

'Get yourself up, today the Lord day.'

The car was made ready and the two women sat side by side in thick sweaty silence for the long ride to the chapel.

The Minister seemed too aware of Desmie's presence. His sermons always seemed to be directed at her.

'Those who have fallen into wickedness. Those who are weak and have not taken the counsel of their elders. Those who are taken in fornication and adultery. They will feel the vengeance of the Lord.'

Then came the murmurs of assent from the congregation.

'For strait is the gate and few there are that can enter therein.'

The congregation consisted mainly of women. Mostly weary and mostly poor. Their men were at home (or someone's home) recovering from Saturday night.

They were easy conquest for the minister. They came either from guilt or the desire for private prayer in a public place.

When young, the girls chased men. When old, they chased God, or the servant of God who was the minister. They could sit quietly in the once-weekly dignity and reflect on the perfect hopelessness of their lives. They could enlist Christ as a fellow conspirator and beg him for vengeance on those who had betrayed them. Some prayed for their men to stop beating them. Some prayed for paralytic stroke to come on an unfaithful lover. Some old women prayed for their children who had long since forgotten them to be punished in their far off countries.

Young women prayed for their bellies to abort the unwanted child. Some prayed for a safe delivery.

The private God in a public place listened to them all.

When the service was done, the women would return home singing the hymns which made the greatest impression on them. Mother Frances loved the hymns. She would use them in her campaign. Now that she did not speak, she would hum or drone softly for hours on end. When she knew that the girl least expected it, she would suddenly burst forth in full voice:

'This is my story
This is my song
Praising my saviour all the day long.'

Sunday evenings were spent in the parlour listening to 'Radio Paradise' on the wireless at full volume. The speakers would beseech the listeners to kneel before their radios, whereupon Mother Frances would go down in the middle of the floor.

Desmie would try to keep to her room on these occasions, but that soon became too suffocating. The tomb too obvious. If she sat on the porch she would feel the lurking eyes of Perkins on her. He daily became more bold with his leering laugh. There was little she could do about it since he never came right out and called her 'whore'.

Since the day of revelation when Mother Frances threatened to cast her out, Perkins had made it his business to be her watchdog. His eyes seemed to say, 'Well, what has become of the untouchable lady with all her hundred dresses? What happened to Miss-Too-Nice?'

She played the piano more these days. The instrument for solitude. It needed tuning but the old lady was in no hurry to have it done. There was a kind of delight in hearing the despair of broken pedals. The desperation of strained strings. This too was part of the punishment.

Why did the old woman hate her so? It was more than disappointment. Did she really want to break her?

Dr Edwards came to visit her in the fifth month. He said that everything seemed to be moving smoothly. Desmie looked at him with disgust. She felt him to be just another conspirator. She wrote in her notebook. This was all she had now.

April 4th
They are all eyes and whispers. They want me to break. Dr E says I must get more exercise. He says I'm getting too heavy, I should walk. Walk where? Mother won't let me be seen on the road. My dresses no longer fit. I wonder if they put a curse on me. This thing in my belly feels like a hot stone.

April 10th
I know now why she hates me. For all the years her husband lived he never saw her naked. Never once. She never liked men. She never had joy. She hates the joy in me.

April 11th
There are only three types of women here on the island. Little girls, dangerous women and old mothers. I'm too old to be little and too young to be old. I must be dangerous, that's why they hate me.

Downstairs she could hear Mother Frances singing:

'There is a place of quiet rest
near to the heart of God
A place where sin cannot molest
near to the heart of God.'

Then there was a knock at the door. She heard her grandmother answer and the voice of a child speaking in polite whispers. She went outside of the room and walked down the steps. Somehow she could sense that it had to do with her. In any case, any change was welcome.

'Mr Carlton said me must bring this ice for you. Him say for tell Mistress Desmie he send it for her, and for give she this letter.'

The old woman took the letter and told the boy to put the crate of ice in the kitchen.

Desmie walked downstairs. The boy looked at her shyly and went out. Desmie ran after him to give him some change.

'Oh no, Miss, him say I mustn't take nothing from you, him pay me good.'

Desmie chipped off a piece of the ice for the boy and gave it to him to suck. She returned to her Mother Francis who had put the letter inside her apron pocket. The look in her eyes showed that she was in two minds as to whether or not to destroy it.

'Please may I have my letter?'

Mother Frances said nothing but gave her the letter with a gesture of dismissal.

Desmie went up the stairs feeling a moment of triumph. The walls had stopped closing in for a moment and the faces in the mirror stopped grinning at her.

Dear Desmie,

Why have you not answered my letters? I hope you are well. I asked for you at work and they just say that you've taken off sick. Your grandmother sent a message with some fellow name Perkins saying you don't want me to come by you again. I didn't like his tone and had to tell him to watch himself. I couldn't do more because I realize that I'll just make it harder for you.

When I first see you I want you. First I say me like, and then I say me love.

She dressed herself quickly and tried to find a pair of shoes which would not hurt her feet. Her ankles had swollen. She did not stop long to think. Her purse. A shawl. She was going down the stairs now. The old woman looked up from her chair.

'Is where you going now?'

She didn't answer but walked quickly towards the door. Mother Frances sprang up.

'Me ask you where you going.'

'You threw away his letters.'

'Yes, me throw dem way. I tell you I don't want you deal with that damn scamp again.'

Desmie went out the door.

'Come back here, Desmie.'

She kept walking forward.

'I say come back here. If you go out you stay out.'

The girl walked the road leading to the town. All she was hearing was voices inside her head. The heat soon made her perspire. Walking was slow and difficult now. She wiped the sweat from her forehead but could not stop it from getting into her eyes and causing tears.

There was a blur and she could not dissociate the voices in her head from the peering faces of people looking out from their yards. She suddenly became aware of people calling after her and laughing.

'Oh God, they're laughing after me,' she thought. 'Why did I come out here. I shouldn't care who laughs at me. But what if he doesn't intend for me to live with him? What if there's someone else there? He might not even be home. Girl, you're foolish. You too foolish.'

Still, she could not stop herself from walking on into the uncertainty. How many houses would she have to pass before she reached the town?

Some children stopped in the road and stared at her. She had the scent of the peculiar and the wounded. The children could sense there was something desperate there. Something they could make ring-songs about. Something they could hear their mother gossiping about over the zinc fences at foreday morning. So they turned to stare and record.

The dizziness started in her head then. The earth was coming up to her more now so it wasn't such an effort walking. It was as if with each step the hot dust of the road was lulling her to fall down and rest. She sensed more than heard the car coming up beside her. She looked up and saw the leering face of Perkins.

'You grandmother say I must come fetch you.'

'No, I'm not going back there.'

'You look tired, girl, come, get in the car and don't make no scene here where these people can laugh after you.'

She felt the weariness overtake her. It was no good arguing. She entered the car and leaned back deep against the seat. She would not let them see her cry. They were in their nakedness and would let the sun dry their tears. She could not.

So she made do with silence and the inward stillness of suffering. Three months passed and the child within her made itself known. Now it was not only silence but pain. The habit of its inward kicking. The certainty of constant being.

Desmie would talk to the thing which moved inside her. As the months passed Mother Frances started to soften and accept the inevitable. She prepared for its coming. She knitted baby clothes in the evening and her singing became less vengeful. In her secret place she never really hated the baby. It was the lack of shame which caused her to weep. She could not admit to Desmie that she too had given birth to her own daughter in exactly the same manner. Had lain with a soft-spoken man with steady hands who made her giddy with his touch and dropped seeds into her as smoothly as water into a vessel. And how she too had to take flight from the whisperings and those who pointed.

It was a ritual among the black poor to play the game of morality. A game played by servants who imitated their masters and who, because they had less, tried to act as if they had more. Yet everyone on the island was related in some way or other. Many married their own sisters or made babies with them, and were none the wiser. But guilt was an important factor in the fabric of island life. It gave something to do while waiting for the resurrection.

Mother Frances had committed one indiscretion. She bore one child out of wedlock and so made a covenant with God never to succumb to the will of the flesh again. Perhaps Desmie too would see the light.

As the months passed she allowed Carlton to visit the house.
To sit in the parlour and catch the scent of lime from the
garden. Desmie was as glad as she was shocked by this
concession. They sat together, the three figures. The eldest
in her rocking chair, observing. Suddenly the old woman
spoke.

'I don't think we ever see you in church.'

Carlton swallowed and reached for another piece of sugar
cake.

'No, M'am.'

'You not a believing man then?'

'Oh, I believe in some things, M'am.'

'Heaven?'

'Yes, M'am.'

'Hell?'

'Yes, M'am.'

'And you does know the difference between the two?'

Desmie jumped in between the two, knowing that the old
woman was setting a trap.

'Mother, of course he — '

'He can speak for himself.'

'Yes, M'am, I know the difference. Hell is what we live
and heaven is what we dream.'

He reached for another rock candy from the bag which he
had brought. He had much experience with pregnant
women and knew what it was that they enjoyed eating.

Mother Frances stopped her rocking.

'Well, make me tell you something, young man. Heaven
and hell is real to me, and no set of cute talk is ever going to
change my mind. I know what is wrong and what is right;
and before my granddaughter met you she know it too. So if I

can't see you in the church then I don't want for see you in me yard, you understand. I want this child for Christian when it born, and they no christening no child if the father and mother no there. You hearing me good?'

'Yes, M'am.'

And so the silence returned. After some time passed Mother Frances looked at her granddaughter, stood up and said: 'Is because he don't believe. That's why he cause green lizard to run up you leg.' Then she went out of the room.

Carlton sat and did not look directly at Desmie, but he could feel her eyes on him and through him.

'I would never hurt you, you know that.'

'I know it, yes.'

'And I would never do nothing to hurt the child. My son, I mean.'

'And how you know it will be a boy?'

'Must be a boy, yes, only make man-child.'

'Oho.'

He smiled wickedly. 'Remember when I first love you what you said?'

She thought for a while, then she smiled too.

'I said take time with me do.'

'Yes. You did fraid me?'

'I never fraid you.'

She started the victrola and played the new record he had brought for her. She knew that soon Mother Frances would appear again in the room. She didn't care. She loved music and for the last few months it was as if she were in mourning. No music had been heard in the house except for the whining of the piano. The record played and drowned out the sound of crickets in the yard.

'One more candle for the wedding cake
and a bottle of cola wine.'

'Maybe you should of fear me,' Carlton said mysteriously.
He knew the girl had never known the kind of violence he
grew up with. She was at home with cotton, silk and bibles,
whereas he knew cards and crap-shooting, knives and
pursuit.

'Mother Frances hate me.'

'Well, you can't blame her, she thinks you spoiled me for
life. Maybe she's right.'

'She hangs around like a John Crow bird sitting in a
duppie tree.'

'She has her ways, but she's still my grandmother.'

'If she could work obeah she'd have me dead, one time.'

The music played:

'It is a wonder, a perfect wonder
What they were dancing in that bar-room last night.'

'Just one thing I ask of you Carlton — '

She watched a candle-fly strike against the lamp and
perish.

'What's that?'

'Be there with me when the child come.'

He was used to this. The others had asked it of him. She
was not so different after all.

'Sure, girl, I'll be with you.'

And she took his hand and rubbed it against her swollen
belly and tried to take the heat of him inside her.

August, the month of heavy rain. It was the end of August

that the new life broke free from inside her. It was not an easy birth. The pains came in earnest. The midwife could not help, nor Mother Frances and all her wisdom. It was as if the thing inside her decided that it would claim the earth now, at this time. She felt herself angry at its insistence. It had taken her over and she was no longer giving birth to it. It was giving birth to her.

The doctor was summoned when the midwife grew frightened. It started by night at eight o'clock under a half moon. The pain came in spasms but no birth. Only pain and greater pain.

She screamed, first into the pillow and then outward into the night. The women came and went, passing through the room in a vigil.

The spasms kept up until the morning. Dr Edwards came, looking sombre. He had his pipe and brown leather bag, both of which his wife had brought back from England for him. He had known Desmie from childhood. He realized that he had trouble on his hands now.

'It's because she hasn't had enough exercise. You should have made her walk. I tell you to get her out of the house.'

Mother Frances put her arms akimbo at her waist.

'And if she don't want for walk, what I must do?'

'You keep her locked up like a prisoner in the house. It's not good.'

'Me no keep nobody no prisoner. If she want walk she could walk.'

'Well, now I have to take her to hospital. Nothing more can be done here. There's a good chance she'll lose the baby.'

'Oh God, no.'

The old woman put her hand on her forehead. Nothing

could be worse than the death of a child in the house. It was a sure sign of curse.

They took her in the car to hospital. By now she no longer cared about anything except the stopping of pain. What was happiness? Happiness was the absence of pain. Nothing more need be given her in life and she would be glad. She prayed in earnest now. Aloud, for it did not matter. Twelve hours it had been, but it seemed eternal.

'God, if you take this pain from me. If you stop the misery —'

It was as if something was ripping her apart from the centre of herself.

'Lord, is it a curse you put on me for loving this man?'

By afternoon she screamed so loudly that she could not hear her voice any longer. It sounded to her as if someone else was screaming. The nurses on the ward looked like John Crow birds. She could not make out their faces, only the grim green of their uniforms. They had no mercy, they had seen too many births.

'Oh God, please give me something to stop the pain.'

They looked down at her and held her legs apart.

'Cho, if you didn't want the pain you should of never slept with he.'

'Oh God, take me, let me die.'

'Yes, girl, you bawling now but it did taste sweet to you when he come inside there, no true?'

And so they taunted her in pairs, taking turns at her. She wanted to spit at them but she had no strength left.

'I think it coming now. Push, girl.'

'I can't, I can't.'

'Quit you bawling and push.'

'Oh God, oh God.'

'Look his head big, eh. Come, girl, is you time now.'

Then it started to happen. She was split open. It seemed to her that it was coming from within her and in that instant one thought alone came to her mind: the striking of lightning in the heavy airless field just when a storm begins. The sudden flashing of lightning which went to her womb and the scream which was not her scream but that of the others. And she lost consciousness then. And she, dreaming, said again and again: Take time with me do. Take time with me.

When she came to they brought the child to her and said it was hers. And she looked down at it but it seemed strange to her.

'May I keep it?'

The nurses looked at her and laughed.

'Of course you can keep it, is yours.'

But she seemed not to believe. It seemed a very small baby to have caused so much pain. She whispered to it: 'Is you that make so much bother?' And then she tried to figure whether or not she hated it. It came of the father, Carlton, but Carlton was not there. And why was he not there as he had promised? Perhaps they never told him, or perhaps he really did not care.

'Well, take him,' said the nurse who had forced her legs open. She remembered her looking down with all that green in her uniform.

Desmie was frightened to take it. It seemed so small and brittle. And where were its eyes? Would it know her, who it had made suffer so anonymously.

Tiny hands grabbed a breast and a mouth found its way to the nipple. Desperate and complete, and all questions were answered. Carlton had said he only made man-children.

The sound of a child's wilderness scream. But what was one scream among so many?

Mother Frances made plans. The time for insults and punishment was over. She now set about securing the way for her new heir's succession. One thought only repeated itself in her head. 'A man-child. Someone who will carry my name.'

From the time the child was brought home the life of the house and all the land which surrounded it changed. It was as if the walls knew, and the crossbeams. The shutters and the porch steps. The grass was freshly cut and the garden tended with a vigilance never seen before. Perkins found little time to drink his rum during the day. The old woman rose at five and inspected every inch of ground. Perkins merely muttered, 'Lord, she in me rass again.'

A room was made ready for the child (Master Legion Rudie Barzey). Two girls were employed as nannies to make certain he never touched earth except with love. If he were ever found to be wet, hungry or unwashed, the girls were made to tremble.

Desmie looked on in greater and greater silence and confusion. She was aware only that she had given birth. As to the implications and repercussions, she did not have a clue. In the beginning the unborn baby was an inconvenience. Then it became a habitual friend in the solitary confinement of scandal to which her grandmother exiled her within the house. In the last months of the pregnancy it became more than a habit, more than occasional kicks and movement. It took her over. By the time of the birth she was terrified of it. Now something different was happening. It was as if the child had taken over the house and completely replaced her.

Mother Frances took little time in making plain the fact that Legion would be her responsibility, not Desmie's. The old woman would insist on seeing him first thing in the morning and the last thing which her eyes would see before sleeping at night would be him (or 'himself' as they called him). When she lay down she would hold conversations with his spirit. She could barely wait until the time when he would be old enough to understand the most important word in his life. 'Land.' Everything, every moment of her remaining life would be to make secure that inheritance.

He must be made to understand. This was the thing from which he had come. The mangoes, cotton, sugar cane. The house. All were part of his inheritance. Perhaps he would have to kill to keep it. Her granddaughter was too foolish ever to understand these things. It was not even worth the trouble to try and explain to her.

At first the girl was glad for the seeming change which had come over the old woman. She felt at peace now that the child was accepted.

'Mother, tell me something.'

'Yes?'

'Why you give me such a hard way to go when you hear I was making baby? Now the baby come you won't even let meself touch him. Fly can't pitch on him.'

'Girl, you too foolish. What I could have do? You did want me let you go sleep with any and every man?'

'No, I didn't expect that but — '

Mother Frances lit her pipe and started to rock back and

forth in her chair.

'But what?'

'You didn't have to treat me so bad. You make me feel I want to dead. You even drive my man away.'

'Me drive him way? Him no damn good anyway, him a scamp.'

The argument was pierced suddenly by the cry of the child. It brought them to consciousness. The concern in the old woman's face and the sound of footsteps of the two girl helpers running through the house to quickly comfort the child lest they be fired.

And so, silently, Desmie became the third member of the house.

THE PRINCE

Time happened between the lime trees, and the young girls bent over him carrying a scent of guava. They dressed him and washed him each in turn. The days were filled with his calling and games beneath the stairs. Evenings always led to Mother Frances' room and long ghostly tales and sugar cake. They called him 'Master Legion' and they smiled. 'How is Master Legion today?' They carried him with them to market and he heard their gossip. He came to know certain trees and roads which led to the house that they told him was his. His house and his land. From the top of the great hill he could see the sea but could not hear it. He began to wonder if that too was his.

Then one Sunday in the spring of the year they put him in the car which Perkins drove and said he must not be frightened. They drove down to the river. There were women dressed in long white dresses and he too wore white. They took him up in their arms and began to wade out into the river. They chanted and waited for the tide and he looked from one face to another but none had his Mother Frances' face. He looked to see if by seeing he could tell which mood they had for him and what was their desire. And they placed

him beneath the water which tasted of greyness and foam.
And he thought perhaps they would not bring him up again.

'The river bed come down
The river bed come down
The river come down
And the dead turning over.'

And when he came up again the faces looked quite
different and it was then that fear left him and they said he
was baptised.

The water made swirls of foam about the women's legs.
The bright whiteness of their dresses stuck tightly around
their round bottoms. Their souls laboured towards God but
their bodies were exposed to the hands of man. The boy
clutched tightly and they pulled him upward from Death.

The old woman watched the boy as he climbed the porch
steps. She enjoyed the muscles in his thin legs. He looked
good in the short pants she had bought for him. She saw the
man he would be. He told her secrets. Came to her for stories
and rewards. Was sly and agile and always running. She
loved him as she had never loved.

Meanwhile Desmie watched him slip from her. At first she
was too busy to notice. She kept watch over her body. Made
note of the stretch marks and swelling of her belly and
wondered how long before she would regain her figure. Her
breasts were still sore from his teeth and savage sucking
when she determined never to have another child. Not that
she did not love the boy, but somehow it took too much out of
her. She wanted to do as she had seen others do with their

children. Nurse them and keep them close but somehow there was no need with all the helpers around her. It seemed to make sense that her grandmother should take charge. After all, what did she know about diaper rash and colic? She was not able to get up all hours of the night with him. She wanted to resume her life where she left off. After the first five months she tried to get back her job at the bank.

'What wrong with you, girl, you drunk? How you could just go back so?'

'But Mother, I don't see why not.'

'Don't you think people know you make a baby?'

'And what if I make a baby, I'm not the first.'

'And what people going say?'

And so she did not go back to the bank. She stayed home for another three months, and by then the feeling of uselessness made her want to scream. The old woman looked at her and realized that something would have to be done before the girl brought new problems to her door.

Letters were secretly written and sent abroad. Arrangements were being made and all the time nothing was either said or asked.

Soon the child didn't know who to call mother. He seemed to feel safer with her grandmother. Desmie made some attempts to bribe some affection from him with sweets and toys but she soon surrendered, realizing at last that Mother Frances had completely taken the child from her.

She started visiting Stephanie and other girlfriends, staying away three and four days at a time. One day she confessed to Stephanie, 'Girl, I don't know, it's like I'm a stranger to my own child.'

'Don't worry, be glad that you don't have to cook and

clean up after him. At least this way you still have you freedom. You not tied down.'

'But freedom to do what?'

Stephanie looked at her surprised. 'Freedom to do whatever you want. You still young. You still have your looks. You could get by. What is it you want to do?'

It was then that the terror struck her. There was nothing that she wanted to do. To the right of her, nothing; to the left of her, nothing. It had all been done either to her or for her. It was the scheme which others had. What she had was the waiting. To wait was the word and the word was made flesh in her.

Now six years had passed. It was the day when Legion battled with Solo which decided Mother Frances. He had come home and stood lizard-still by the door. She had turned and seen him.

'If you have a mother then you must have a father.'

'What?'

'Is who my father?'

'Why you asking me?'

He would not answer.

'Alright, you want to know? You father was a candle man.'

'Candle man? So where he now?'

'Gone way. Ship take him.'

'And how they call him?'

'They call him Barzey, just like you.'

'Oh, then is his name I have.'

'Of course.'

'Will I ever see him?'

'No,' she said, turning away. 'He gone far.'

Well, he thought, at least I have his name. But she knew that the lie would not hold him for long. He was asking questions now.

Something was going on in Mother Frances' mind. What it was exactly was not clear, but Desmie noticed a change in the old woman.

At first there was a series of long letters written to America. Mother Frances would usually have asked Desmie to write them for her as she did not trust either her eyes or her own spelling. Desmie was not asked. Instead, Mother Frances would make long trips into town to see 'someone on business'. The someone-on-business turned out to be a lawyer named Daley. A man of forty who was built like a wine bottle (he had a large round body and a small head) and still lived with his mother.

What bothered Desmie was that she was made to feel like a child who could not be confided in. Mother Frances let slip the fact that what she was doing had something to do with Desmie's future. Perkins, the gardener-chauffeur, seemed aware. Now his obnoxious grin seemed broader than ever. Desmie wondered if perhaps her grandmother was making out a will. Why else would she go and see a lawyer. Surely if she were making out a will it would have more to do with the boy than with her. It was clear that Mother Frances cared only for the boy and that she, Desmie, had fulfilled whatever function she had. One day the old woman came to her room. She seemed pleased with herself.

'Well, everything is in order.'

'What's in order, Mother?'

'You're going to live in the States.'

Desmie looked in disbelief at the old woman. Could she be serious?

'To live in the States . . . but how I could — '

'Your aunt agree to sign the papers for you to come over.'

'But how about Legion?'

The old woman's face suddenly became hard: 'He'll stay here with me for now.'

Something did not seem right. It was too sudden, too unprepared.

'But I can't just leave the boy.'

'How you mean, you just can't leave him? I say I will take care of him. Be glad you getting a next chance.'

Somehow the words 'a next chance' sounded more like a sentence than an opportunity. She suddenly found her heart racing. She went outside to where she heard the boy playing. She was frightened now and she had the feeling that he was vanishing before her eyes. She called him and tried to keep the stammer out of her voice. When she turned she saw the old woman standing behind her.

'Come here, Legion. How would you like to stay with Mother Frances here?'

The boy looked confused. He looked from one face to another.

'How you mean?'

'You mother going away for a while and so it's just going to be the two of we here.'

The boy looked into his mother's face to see if she would say anything. When nothing came he turned again to Mother Frances.

'You go stay and protect me? Make sure nothing happen to me?'

'Yes, M'am, I go stay.'
Now Desmie looked from her grandmother's eyes to the
boy's. The eyes no longer seemed innocent.

There's a conspiracy, she thought. They've already
worked it all out without me. He knew. They all knew and
didn't tell me. They're playing a game with me and I've
already lost him forever.

The boy pressed himself against the old woman's dark
dress. He looked at his mother and saw a stranger.

Things moved quickly after that. Within a month all the
arrangements were made. Tickets were provided for the
journey and several trunks were purchased and made ready
for Desmie's departure.

The people on the island loved departures more than
arrivals. Any departure, be it for death or for parts unknown.
Many clothes were given away to servant girls and what was
not given was begged for. It was the custom. The girls
preferred wearing the second-hand clothes even to being
given new ones. It was almost like a wake, this going. Even at
the farewell party they sat about wearing Desmie's panties
and dresses. The shoes were kept for Sunday. It was well
known that Desmie seldom wore a dress more than twice.
Many of the girls were called upon to distribute their
new-gotten clothes to others who were jealous of their good
fortune. This way the clothes spread throughout the whole
island and became the topic of conversation. It was as if it
were the body and blood of the slain Christ.

They made sure to take her address in the States for as
soon as she arrived there would be letters begging aid or

assistance to help them cross over to the New Jerusalem.

Even her friend Stephanie seemed a little strange, as though she too resented her breaking free.

'Well, I guess you will soon forget all about us, girl.'

'No, of course not, Stephanie, I'm not going to forget you.'

'Well, anyway, I'll soon be going from this graveyard too.'

But there was a coldness in her eyes which Desmie had never seen before.

As she was packing she came across Gladstone's poem:

'And how shall I approach my love
Whose stillness is like the sky above
And how shall I take her hand
I who am but a lonely man?'

How stupid he was, full of poetry and small island politics. But when he came to see her he brought his sad serious face which made her feel guilty for almost destroying his poem.

He seemed to have resolved something in his mind now that he knew she was leaving and might never return. He asked to take her for dinner and then out dancing. Mother Frances seemed to approve of this outing. Desmie wanted to tell him no, but it seemed heartless as she may never see him again.

There were few places one could go to for an evening out. The routine was pretty well established. There were few places where 'nice' girls went with men. The aim was to spend money and sip from brightly coloured drinks. They went to the Colony Club which served a drink called Pina Colada. The place was mellowed by the flickering candles on each table and the sound of the sea could be heard nearby.

The place was patronized mostly by tourists but had lately become accessible to the islanders.

Desmie looked at the shifting face of Gladstone as he bent across the table towards her. She kept drifting in and out of his voice. She wished that he wouldn't speak so much and just let her enjoy one of the last few nights she would have at home.

Yes, the Colada was good. She began to feel that she should be kinder to him, he was a good person after all, just not very —

He was saying something which ended in a question. Oh yes, he wanted to dance: that must be why he had extended his hand towards her.

The music was all right, something romantic. They moved together across the floor. He danced very correctly, the way he did everything else. Now he was talking again. She smiled and tried to concentrate on the music. Even now he wouldn't hold her too tight. She wondered what he would do if she put her head like this on his shoulder. He seemed very surprised. There, he's stopped talking.

Suddenly, through the room's flickering, she recognized a girl she once worked with at the bank. Estelle Gooding. She recognized her from her back, the way she held her head. She could not see who she was dancing with but somehow she sensed more than saw him and she knew with certainty that it was him. She felt off balance.

Carlton came over to the table. She had tried to avoid looking over in their direction. She tried as best she could to get involved in the stupid chatter that was Gladstone's conversation. But she knew he would come over. It was

Gladstone who first looked up and saw him. Then in the silence which followed Desmie felt a tightening in the back of her neck which moved slowly down between her shoulder blades. This was always where the tension would grip her first.

'Hello, so you're here. I heard you leaving.'

He had some nerve coming to her table like this, acting as though Gladstone did not even exist.

'Gladstone, this is Carlton; Carlton, Gladstone. I don't know if you've met.'

The two men looked at each other.

'Would you like to dance?'

'I've just been dancing. I feel sort of hot now.'

'The breeze will cool you.'

Already he was lifting her to her feet. She was angry at his arrogance. She didn't want to make a scene because she knew that would have been to his advantage.

'Excuse me, Gladstone, you don't mind if I — '

'No, of course not,' he stammered.

Then they were inside each other's arms and it seemed too quick and too natural as if it were only a continuation. The way he held her, it was too evident that they were familiar.

She looked across the room and saw Estelle staring. She was trying to ignore them but kept looking over her shoulder at them.

'You look good. Motherhood must agree with you. It fill you out.'

'Really.'

'So you're going to go away?'

'You shouldn't hold me so tight.'

'Why?'

'Because I didn't come with you and you didn't come with

me. Estelle looks jealous.'

'Someone will soon ask her to dance.'

'That's how you treat your women, isn't it.'

'You was going to run away and not see me?'

'I wasn't running, I was walking.'

'You could just forget so?'

'The music's stopped.'

But she did not make any attempt to free herself from him. 'It will start again.'

As they danced the next dance she began to feel guilty. Gladstone deserved better than this. It was he who had brought her. He would never forgive her.

When the music ended she made her way abruptly back to her table without bothering to give the perfunctory thank you which women said on the island when a dance finished.

She was surprised when Carlton brought Estelle to the table and suggested they make a foursome of it. Gladstone was out of his element. He did not know what to say to avoid it. He would have liked to have said something but he knew that Carlton was not above fighting in public. Right there in the middle of the Colony Club floor, sending Pina Coladas and other guests sprawling. Somehow Gladstone sensed that this was the sort of fellow who would carry a knife and use it. He soothed his hurt pride with the fact that Estelle was not bad looking at least.

They sat and talked for some time, drinking and trying to make the best of an awkward situation. Desmie decided to ask to be taken home.

Carlton insisted on a last dance.

Estelle was asked by Gladstone. It was some time before they noticed that Carlton and Desmie had left.

It was a humid night and everything felt close and conspiratorial. They drove up into the hills. There was a breeze there. She felt guilty about leaving Gladstone. She would not have done such a thing normally, although she would have wanted to. Now here she was with the man who had caused her to leave the island. She told herself that it was wrong but she felt so comfortable beside him.

She tasted of Pina Colada and he tasted of rum and sweat, and when he kissed her the third time he tasted of blood where she had bitten his lip. He was the father of her child. They could not blame her for making love with him again. But they would blame her for they would surely know. The breeze felt so good and calming. She had only meant to stay an hour but could not leave him until dawn.

They'll hang you as much for an hour as for a night, she thought.

He made love to her in the car at first. She felt strange there, but good. Then he drove to his house and he wanted her there for the last time. She knew the bed and the window which faced the garden. She could scream into his shoulder and feel the muscles along his legs. Take what mercy she could from the mattress. Come up and meet his body and challenge him until he drove her backward into a quivering.

She told herself this would be the last time and she would have to make do with memory, then she would get up and wash his seed out of her forever.

Dawn surprised them, coming easy between the houses along the hill. He was amazed that he was not tired and still wanted to make love to her again.

'I could keep going and never stop, you know, girl.'

But she knew it was only because she was leaving.

'If we live together you would soon get tired though. You'd make love one time and snore.'

'Never happen.' He laughed and bit her left breast which was larger than the right.

She knew that if she did not leave now she would never leave. He would win her beyond all reasoning. So she put his hands away from her and went to bathe.

They did not speak on the way to her house. They listened to the sound of the village waking. The sound of the farmers on their way to market. Babies crying and old women singing hymns as they started their washing. She suddenly thought to herself, My God, I'll miss this place. So dirty and so small and filled with gossip and dying, but I will miss it.

When she reached home the old woman was up. She did not know what she would say to Mother Frances. The woman looked at her for a long time in silence.

'Is now you come. I could smell you. Well, anyway, praise God you leaving tomorrow.'

'Is . . . the boy awake?'

'Why you want know?'

Desmie did not bother to answer her but walked instead upstairs to his room.

'Left him alone. Is where you was?'

There was a word on Desmie's lips but she forced it back between her teeth and walked instead to her room and let the tiredness take her. She could still feel him inside her. For now they could not have that.

She did not wake until five in the afternoon. She looked from her window into the garden and the leering grin of Perkins' eyes as they stared up at her. She felt herself violated and withdrew suddenly from the window. He seemed happy with himself for having caught her at that moment, then returned to stroking the car engine.

She began to see to the packing. The suitcase she would carry aboard ship. Everything else had already been sent on. She looked at several photographs of the boy. One she especially liked was of him in a sailor suit. He already looked certain and self-assured like his father. What if she would never see him again? But no, that would be impossible. They could not do that to her. She would let her grandmother have her little victory for now, but as soon as she got herself situated in the States she would send for him. She packed the dress she wore last night. When she reached the States she would take it out to remind her.

The room looked quite empty now. It was only herself to be removed and then the silence would set in. She felt hungry but was not up to seeing Mother Frances just yet. She listened for the sound of the boy's voice but couldn't hear it. Perhaps she had taken him out. That was it. She would not want him to be too close to her now. Mother Frances thought of everything.

Desmie turned and looked at the walls of her room. The walls which had witnessed everything. Her birth, her childhood, her first period. Her first real lover. She would miss this room and yet she hated its closeness. She heard a voice calling her name.

'Desmie, you up?'

'Yes, Mother.'

'Not even the Queen self does sleep all day.'

'I was just packing.'

She looked down the stairs and into the disbelieving eyes of Mother Frances.

The old woman had been busy. She made certain that all was made ready and that nothing was left to chance. The car had been prepared. The sum of money, four hundred dollars, had been drawn out and placed in an evelope. A blue envelope which she had especially bought from the Assyrian's shop in town. In another envelope she had very carefully written a letter in a large unsteady hand which was nevertheless very readable and to the point:

> Mr Carlton,
> If you make any attempt to see my granddaughter or at any time or place try to interfere with her son, I will see to it that you die.
> I will not send anyone after you, I will do it myself because I am an old woman and have nothing to lose.
> Yours,
> Mrs Frances. Cork Hill

When Carlton received the letter he laughed at first, but his hands grew cold. She was a strange woman but a serious one and he felt with some certainty that she meant it. They were the same somehow. Different from Desmie, not full of dreams and wonder, but hard and pulled out of the earth. She was both fire and ice, calm and deadly. No, he would stay out of her way for now.

Mother Frances rose early this morning. She always rose early but today she rose especially early. This was the day of her granddaughter's leaving and therefore it would have to be orchestrated carefully.

The breakfast was made ready. The necessary documents placed on the cupboard. Only then did she wake Desmie. All was well planned. The boat was leaving at eight. Desmie never liked to wake early. She would need plenty of time to orient herself. Everything must be prepared.

Somehow Mother Frances had the feeling she would never see her again in this life. The thought did not bother her particularly. She had no further use for the girl. The boy had been produced; that was all that was necessary. Thank God she was not poor like most of the people of the island. The widowed and broken women or the muttering old men who slept only by rum and tears, lamenting the fact that their children wouldn't even bring them a crust of bread or a cup of water, when, of course, neither bread nor water was what they wanted, but money was. No, this was not Mother Frances' fate. She turned to knock on wood. All she wanted was someone who was strong and not ignorant enough to waste the land which she had struggled so many years to acquire. Land which was so hard to come by. Land which the slaves were never allowed to own. Now she possessed it and now with the grace of God she had someone to pass it to.

Desmie was a fool. That was a given fact. The girl was weak since she never had to struggle for anything. She didn't even know how to keep her legs closed when a man came courting, but well — never mind. All was for the best.

With these thoughts Mother Frances mounted the stairs and pushed open the door to the girl's room. She wanted to say: Wake up you foolish girl and leave this place before you cause me new scandal. Instead she said:

'Desmie, come on, girl, time to come eat.'

There was much to do. She wanted to go and talk with the boy. Mother Frances said it was best just to kiss him and go quickly.

'Don't disturb him, it may make him cry.'

It seemed the best course. She knew if she looked at him too long she would again see Carlton's face and find herself rooted to the spot. She had to leave quickly. It was her only chance of freedom.

She left the room first with her mind and then with her body.

THE BETRAYAL

Legion Rudie Barzey went down the long path which led
from school. He felt a kind of buzzing in his head. Since the
woman who they said was his mother had left, he felt a
strangeness whenever he heard someone mention her name.
It was strange because he had never really thought of her as
anything more than a boarder in the house. She might have
been an older sister or perhaps a cousin. She sometimes
scolded him but her anger had no authority. It was as if she
did not know how to be angry. It was always Mother Frances
who decided what he would wear or when he would eat.
When the shoes came from America for him, she felt
compelled to say: 'Is you mother send these for you.' And yet
there was a dismissive gesture which she made with her
hands. A kind of understatement in her voice as if to say:
'What could that fool ever know about shoes.' The insult was
never stated but implied. And yet something was not quite
right about the woman's absence. Something in the equation
of life was slightly off.

He talked to his friend Solo about it as they walked the
long dirt road which led to town. He in his new shoes and
Solo barefoot.

'You know me mother gone?'

Solo walked along slowly as he always did. Half of his bottom was showing through the worn khaki shorts he wore. He acted at first as though he had not heard.

'How you mean she gone?'

'She gone America.'

'And so what's that to you?'

'Well, it feel funny.'

'Cho man, what's a mother? Me never know me mother. A mother is anybody who feed you when night come.'

'And how about father?'

The boy looked at him for the first time.

'You forget what I tell you about how dog and rooster fuck?'

'No, I don't forget.'

'Well then, a father is anybody who sleep with you mother. A father is a man who cut you ass if you beg him for money, or if he drink too hard.'

'That is a father?'

'So it really be. You not missing nothing.'

The two walked on into silence.

So his mother, Desmie, had fled and left him. She had fled the boredom of the island. Fled repeated pregnancies and women and cousin Clarke who smelled of talcum powder and sweat. And now Mother Frances had him to herself. He did not really mind this for he was more spoiled than ever. So the state of things flowed. From rainy season to Christmas and Carnival time with its masked jumbies and the sweet smell of pig roasted on a spit.

He had become accustomed to the expressions which the servant girls used as they looked after him:

'Master Rudie born with a silver spoon in he mouth.' He had never seen the silver spoon but came to believe in its existence. There was no reason to fear and no cause to doubt. Everything which existed was for him. The first light of the sun and its setting. The shadows which trees made under the moon.

Every month the blue envelopes came from America and he would hear Mother Frances talk to herself and mutter under her breath.

Time, it moved on in an even stream. Running like the rain water along the ridges of the hill which led to the big white house which was his.

There was an endless succession of servant girls who came with small breasts and shy eyes, and left when they became bold and pregnant.

Mother Frances told him things. Not too much but enough to clarify and confuse him. She told him that he was named Legion after the doctor who brought him into the world when he was very sick and no one knew if he would live. She smiled to herself when she talked about the nine days which they watched him and waited to see if he would survive. Nine days and they knew he would be a man.

The boy's eyes looked into her and asked, 'And what about my father?'

'What father? Why you asking about father for?'

'Well, I just wonder if I was name after him. Is he that name me?'

She grew very angry suddenly and began to walk away from him.

'You never mind about you father. Is not him name you, is me who name you Legion after you doctor.'

He knew he was on dangerous ground when he questioned her about anything having to do with his father. He could not keep his mind from wondering. Solo had sparked him off and then there were all those curious stares and whispers which the gossiping women in the church gave. Even the preacher had one day overstepped his mark and asked after his mother. Mother Frances soon held him in check. It was as if no one had anything to do with his birth but herself. She was father and mother both. The boy was told to believe in this as much as the white house which he lived in. The certainty of the trees which grew in the garden.

Then one day she took sick, the old woman, and kept to her room and brought a heavy silence into the house. People would come to visit her and pat the boy on the head on their way in and out of the house. Neighbours would cook food and bring baskets. Mother Frances grew more suspicious and warned against eating the things they brought. The boy was confused. Those who did not bring food brought medicine, things to boil and drink, things to rub, things to inhale, but still she grew more sick. The doctor came, looking tired and grim. He studied the boy from over his glasses, then went upstairs with slow and deliberate steps to Mother Frances' room. He left medicine and advice and studied the boy again on the way out.

'What wrong with Mother Frances, doctor?'

'She have a fever, son.'

'When she come better?'

'Soon, soon.'

And when he went into the darkened room which smelled

familiar of limacol and eucalyptus, he felt afraid when he heard her talking, for when he answered her he realized it was not to him that she spoke.

'We burn the cloth beneath the navel string tree. Nobody will find it. He all right. No one will tief him from me.'

She went on in this way for three days, continuing with what seemed to be a private conversation with a silent host and always there came the refrain:

'And what me for do, Lord? What me for do?'

The boy felt angry that she did not include him. She had never done that before.

It was the third day, when he stopped on his way home from school to pick gladiolas for her. She always loved the scent. He knew that would make her better. He ran so quickly that he cut his leg on a thorn but hardly felt it, running to her. He came into the house, threw his notebook on the table and ran upstairs to her room.

He came up to her bed and she was silent now. He put the flowers close to her face. Tickle her nose with the flowers and wake her. But she did not wake. And then he called her once, then twice, then a third time and she still did not answer. He knew to himself. Having seen chickens which dogs had gotten to. He knew the word death for he had heard and seen it almost from the beginning.

And then he walked and did not run from the room but walked backwards to the door. Because it was still Mother Frances and not a duppie which would harm him.

And when they came, the others, coming first singularly and then together, they started to cry out. And one woman, who was called Mrs Davis though she never married, tore the headtie from her head and cried into her hands.

And someone came and took him from where he sat outside on the steps of the house watching the sliding away of the sun-weary lizards.

The women prepared her body for the earth. She was not foolish and had made everything ready. The dress had already been chosen. Everything put away for this special end.

The island was merciful with its dead. The body must be buried within forty-eight hours because no amount of ice could keep it from stinking. There was therefore little time for sorrow.

That night they held a wake. The women sang. The men drank and talked. Some played cards. Throughout there was food. Some went about the house in search of possessions. They emptied everywhere except the actual room where the body lay. None was bold enough to take from that room. It was known that Mother Frances was well acquainted with obeah. Although no one ever said it aloud, it was known by all. The mirrors were covered in white. The thieving crowd confined themselves to the dishes, sewing machine and silverware.

He came upon them as they took out the heavy silver tray and he looked and watched as they transformed themselves before his eyes. Though he had known them by name, now they became birds. Death birds who had waited this night. He walked up to them suddenly and staring right into one woman's bird-eyes said:

'Mistress Greenaway, put that tray down.'

They looked at him in wonder.

'But how you mean, boy? Mother Frances would have want me have this.'

He looked through her and his eyes did not blink.

'You can't tief it, put it down.'

The woman turned to another.

'But eh eh, look 'pon me wok here. All you see this little boy say me tiefing. Why you don't go you bed?'

'You can't have it I say.'

And when they heard him they couldn't help but grow frightened. His eyes were not a little boy's eyes but eyes like Mother Frances'. Eyes which stared through you but never turned away.

They tried to laugh it off, but no one took that silver tray.

The funeral was a political affair. The local preacher was not allowed to bury her because she had left special instructions that only Reverend Girty could bury her. This caused some embarrassment to the local churches in the parish. Reverend Girty was close to ninety and lived all the way on the other side of the island. He had to be summoned but when he heard that it was Mother Frances he came willingly.

The boy dressed in the long trousers which he wore on special Sundays, and he was made to put on the shoes from America. They hurt his feet but looked respectable. Hiding outside the circle of mourners he saw Solo.

They sang 'In the Sweet By and By' and Reverend Girty read the text which she had written was to be said.

'Lord now let this thy servant depart in peace.'

This soon became the largest funeral ever seen on the island. All the women were satisfied. They turned to each other and said 'Now this *is* a funeral.'

'Just so I want bury.'

'There is a place of quiet rest near to the heart of God.'

They turned to the boy and asked him if he were not frightened. He shook his head but they were not satisfied.

'You not sad, boy?'

'Left him alone no, of course he must be feel sad. No mother here and no grandmother. He must be feel sad.'

Then the thought came to them suddenly: 'What's to become of the boy?'

After the funeral and the death birds came the lawyers. They came to search for papers. The boy locked the door and would not let them in.

'Now see here, boy, we come to help you. Mother Frances say we must look after things.'

But he would not open the doors and they could not decide what to do with him. They left to consult with the police. He felt safe there in the house. He walked about from room to room and watched his shadow on the wall. Then he heard a knocking at the window. He looked from the window upstairs but saw nothing. He went downstairs and crawled on his knees. He heard his name being called.

'Legion, is me, Solo.'

He opened the window and Solo climbed in.

'Is you one here, man?'

'Yes.'

'You not fraid to stay here alone?'

'They trying to get it.'

'Who?'

'They say Mother Frances tell them to look after the house.'

'Don't let the fuckers in. They too tief. I bring a coconut. You want piece?'

The two sat down on the floor and cracked open the coconut. First Solo cut into the eyes to let out the juice and they drank the water which was thick like milk. They laughed together and waited while outside the world made manoeuvres.

After they finished eating Solo sat on the floor and began cleaning his nails with a small penknife he carried. He saw that Legion was deep in thought.

'They're going to come again you know.'

'I know.'

'What you going to do?'

'I won't let them in.'

'They're big people. You can't stop them if they really want come. If you act too hard they put you in boy prison.'

Legion thought about Mother Frances. He could see her looking at him.

'I never go let them take this house from me.'

Solo looked at him and gave a smile of respect.

'You hard yes.'

There was the sound of an approaching car outside. The sound of footsteps bruising the wood of the porch steps. The boys' eyes grew wide. They waited.

'Legion, you in there?'

Silence.

'I know you in there. Stop playing the fool and open this door.'

It was Perkins calling him.

'Come on,' said Solo, 'let's push this table against the door.'

They started pushing.

'I not going tell you again. If you don't open this door, you go get a cut ass today.'

More sounds of whispering and then the voices began to

move and encircle the house. They saw a face staring in through a window. They kept close to the floor.

'Quick, let's check the back door,' said Solo.

They crawled on their knees and came to the back of the house. The side door which led to the wash house had a bolt but it was not drawn. The boy reached it seconds before it was pushed and then kicked. Would they go away now? Suddenly there was a crash and a window shattered, and then Perkins pushed himself through. He breathed heavily from the effort and had the smile of a goat.

When at last he got into the house, Lawyer Daley read out the will. The boy was well provided for. To him belonged the house and the greater portion of land.

Legion would be raised by Mother Frances' sister Anne, who was to be contacted in America. Of Desmie little was said other than to leave it to Great Aunt Anne to decide what her share of the estate should be.

It was Mother Frances' express desire that the care and education of the child should not be left to his mother. It was also clearly stated that Legion's share of the estate was intended solely for him, and that his mother should not benefit from it. Whether or not she married.

Perkins swore that he had been promised a car as well as twelve acres of land approaching a gully.

Others said that land they had rented had been promised to them.

And so there was much murmuring outside the door.

For a day there was great debate as to what to do with the boy. No one had laid a hand on him but Solo was given two slaps and a swift kick which sent him sprawling. This was delivered by Perkins who then made the error of turning his back on the boy and so didn't see with what speed Solo recovered his feet and bent to send a stone which caught Perkins on the side of the head which all but made him unconscious. Solo then vanished into the bush.

Everyone was in favour of waiting for Desmie to come and fetch the boy.

'That Solo go be a bad influence on him, you watch. He soon going come just like some wild animal.'

'That boy a damn scamp, me could tell you.'

The problem of the boy was directly related to the problem of the land and house. There were already many who had an eye on it and were waiting patiently. If perhaps the boy could be sent away then perhaps —

But the happenings of the following day put paid to all speculation.

A large black car moved slowly up the side of the hill. It was not yet midday so the sun was not yet vicious, there was still a bit of breeze after the morning rain. A spider moved easily over the panes of broken glass in the window. Slowly.

When the car reached the front of the white house a woman emerged. She wore black shoes with thick heels. Her hat was cocked to the side. When she emerged from the car the driver ran after her carrying her suitcases and making amiable sounds in the hope of receiving a large tip. She paid him and dismissed him with a gesture of her hand. Each step she took gave an air of importance.

She regarded the small boy seated on the porch steps, his thin legs twining about themselves like a snake. The look she gave him was one of acknowledgment.

'You're Rudie.'

It was less a question than a statement. The boy nodded his head. She swept past him and went inside. Several of the neighbour women who had come to fix food and clean and steal, greeted her but she seemed not to have time for them. Instead, she went straight to Mother Frances' room and closed the door after her. Then there was a long silence which was made heavy by everyone pausing to listen. Then there came the slow rising sound of weeping. It went on for some time and the women all nodded their heads in understanding. None tried to enter the room or disturb her from her private grief. They would not interfere with their sympathy and banalities. One by one they left the house and the small boy sat at his station on the porch steps and waited for the silence to return again.

When she came out she made him stand and then gave her scrutiny.

'I am your Aunt Nam, did Mother Frances tell you of me?'

He did not answer but instead shook his head.

'You mustn't shake your head when I ask a question. You must say no, no, Aunt Nam.'

'No, Aunt Nam.'

'Good, you will soon get to know me.'

'You won't make them take my house, Aunt Nam?'

'And who tell you is your house?'

'Lawyer Daley tell me.'

'Oh, I see. Well, we'll have a long time to speak of that.'

But she did not speak of it. Instead she saw to his dinner and then washed him down and stared at his body in a strange way which made him frightened. She was examining him for something. He could feel her staring. And when she saw his shyness she laughed at him and played with his manness in her hand.

'We'll soon fix that.'

'Fix what, Auntie?'

'You going to have to be circumcised.'

'What that is, Auntie?'

'That is something to make you like a man and not a dog.'

'I don't understand, Auntie.'

'You will come to understand.'

The boy looked at her to see if she was serious. He could not tell. He did not yet know her ways. They were a queer lot, these old people. They would sometimes have you on with their private tight and cruel jokes. And just when you thought they might be laughing they would turn grim. Here was another old and overdressed woman come into his life. She said that they would circumcise him. He could not tell what the word meant but it had a sound to it which said pain. If only there was some way to tell what they meant to do to you, but they were full of secrets, these people. Sometimes they farted and would not say excuse me, though they made him say it, but when they did it they turned their faces away and left you with a smell and a silence which made *you* guilty.

'Why did Mother Frances die, Aunt Nam?'

She looked at him but yet not at him, but at the space around him.

'She died because God wanted her.'

'And does God want me?'

'Yes, of course God wants you.'

'Then am I going to dead too?'

'All of us will die.'

'All, everybody?'

The thought terrified him. It was a sentence, complete

and unescapable.

'Yes son, everybody. Now come eat your food.'

He ate but did not remember eating.

From that night his life seemed to change. He could never feel the same again.

The woman had put her hands on him when he got ready for bed. She slept in the bed with him. He felt strange having her there and yet felt he needed her company. She had put hands on him. Placed a new wall around him. He closed his eyes in the darkness and watched the falling sandlike figures which always pulled him down into sleep.

He had never known fear before, but now he knew fear. That was what she had given him.

He saw himself lying in bed. He stepped outside of himself and saw himself dreaming. He relived the events of the day before. The sounds of scratching and breathing at the door. The breaking of glass. He knew there was something outside which was trying to get him. Could it be God who was a killer, a hunter of those whom he loved? Something outside the door. And then he heard Mother Frances' voice. He had never feared her before, but now it wasn't the Mother Frances he had known but something duppy-like and covered in flowers.

He tried to scream but had no voice. He turned and saw his aunt stretched out beside him. If only he could touch her to wake her but he was paralyzed. He had no hands and no voice and still they kept coming closer. Outside. But now it was inside until finally he knew he too was dying. Then, only then, did the voice escape his throat and he found his scream.

THE LEAVING

It was strange the way everyone knew that he was leaving the island. Long before even he knew. Everyone had taken it for granted the moment that Aunt Nam came.

One day she said, in her asking way, 'Would you like to go to the States with me?'

He tried to catch her eyes to find her meaning but the eyes said nothing. They were only cloudy and distant.

'I don't think so, you know.'

'Yes you would. You will like it there.'

'Why I would like it?'

'Because you can see all the big buildings. Go to school and learn to be a man.'

'But Auntie, I go to school here.'

'Never mind.'

Later that day he was walking home with Solo.

'Auntie say she want take me to States.'

'Me know that long time.'

'How you know?'

'Everybody know.'

'I don't want to go.'

'You have to go. Is why she came for get you. Me wish it

was me. You not go have no time for we again.'

With that Solo walked on ahead of him as though he were angry.

'Why you say that? I can't forget you.'

'You go come a Yankee boy.'

He could see the hatred in Solo's face now.

'I don't want come no Yankee boy. I want stay here with you like always.'

'Go way, nobody need you. I stay by meself. Anyway, you go have to give me something before you go.'

'What I could give you? I have some sea shells you could keep for me.'

'I don't want no puss claat sea shells. Could find sea shells any day.'

'Well, what you want then?'

He had to run after Solo who was a good distance from him now.

'Me want money is what me want.'

Solo turned around with such fury to say these words that his cap dropped from his head. The cap was a wool one which he always wore regardless of the heat of the day. He bent quickly to pick it up. As he dusted it off he tried to keep the slight embarrassment from his face. It was unlucky to have your hat fall to the earth. Usually it meant that someone close to you might fall ill. He looked at the cap in his hand.

Legion thought to himself that Solo resembled Tall-boy in his movements. He had the same rage. He held objects in his hand like a eucharist.

The whole action took only a few seconds. He turned to walk away.

Legion realized in that moment that he did not like his aunt. In the little time since she came she had made nothing but trouble for him. First she had introduced him to fear and nightmares by telling him about God and death. She had transformed the image he had of Mother Frances from friend to ghost. Now she was making enemies for him by taking him away and causing jealousy among his friends. She was dangerous, this strange woman. Better if she had just stayed away and sent blue envelopes from America.

'Okay, Solo, if is money you want I could bring you some.'

Solo turned and looked at him with the clear eyes of suspicion. 'When you going bring it?'

'Tomorrow.'

They walked on together. Neither spoke again.

That night he made his plan. He knew what he must do. He had no nightmare that night. He slept calmly.

In the morning as he dressed for school he looked from his window and saw Auntie outside talking with Perkins. He moved quickly, searching through her suitcase until he found her purse. He opened it and a scent of perfume came out as the lock gave a little click. He took out five dollars and found a silver coin which was large and round. He placed the purse back inside the case. Made the little click again and placed the money inside a kerchief and put it inside his pants pocket. It felt good stealing from the purse, like putting his hand between a girl's legs and smelling it.

She gave him breakfast and checked his clothes for school.

'What's that sticking out you pocket?'

His heart started pounding.

'Nothing, just a kerchief.'

'Well fold it so it doesn't stick out so. You look like a hoodlum.'

'Yes, Auntie, I'm late.'

With that he jumped up and got his school book. She watched him suspiciously as he ran off down the road.

In the afternoon he met Solo and gave him the money.

'Is where you get it from?'

'I get it.'

'You tief it. Me never know *you* could drop stick.'

He answered with silence.

'You all right. Come here and stick out you hand.'

Legion put his hand forward and suddenly felt a sharp pain. Solo cut his finger and then cut his own.

'You fraid?'

'I'm not fraid,' he lied, and tried to keep the tears away from his eyes.

Solo twisted his finger around Legion's so that the blood of the two merged.

'Now we brothers. I never tell and you never tell unless we dead.'

'Unless we dead,' he answered, and looked straight into Solo's eyes.

That night Legion kept quiet. He expected something to happen. Some explosion. None came. The meal was prepared in quiet and taken in guilt. Auntie was too busy with her preparations to take much notice of him.

The explosion came with morning. Morning, when all one's defences are down and the boy was still curved in the foetal position of birth and sleep. A sudden hand reached inside him and roused him from calm.

'Wake up, boy.'

He was climbing on the roof of the house reaching for a mango that was on a far branch; as he stretched for it he started to fall. . .

'Wake up, I say, I know you hearing me.'

He opened his eyes still heavy with sleep.

'What you do with the money?'

'Which money?'

'The money that was in my purse, what you do with it?'

'I never see no money.'

'I know I had a five dollars in there, I meant was to give it to Mistress Daley and now is gone.'

'I never see it.'

'If is not you, then who take it?'

'I don't know. Why you accusing me?'

'Somebody in this house is a tief. All right, I can't be sure is you but you let me ever catch you take something from my purse and you go see what happen. I go do for you. You hear what I'm saying?'

Silence.

'You hear what I'm telling you?'

'Yes.'

(Slap) 'Yes what?'

He held his face. 'Yes, Auntie.'

'Now get washed and ready for school. Today is you last day.'

He jumped out of bed, careful not to meet her flashing eyes which seemed to cut through him like an x-ray machine. He wondered if she could read his thoughts.

He washed quickly. The slap had not hurt as much as the shock. She can't prove it was me, he thought to himself.

He went to put on his trousers for school and found that all his pockets had been turned inside out. He tried to act normal but found that it was not that easy. He ate his breakfast quickly and avoided her eyes which were checking on his from across the room. He felt her come closer.

'Swear to me that you didn't take that money.'

'I swear.'

She went and got a bible. He recognized it. It was Mother Frances'.

'Swear on this bible. You know God will strike you dead if you lie.'

'I know.'

'Swear.'

'I swear.'

He was glad when he ran out of the house down the path and out to freedom. Maybe God would strike him down. If he did it would not be in the day. It would be at night when the duppies walked. He would worry about it later.

He did not mind dying. He did not mind his Mother Frances' death. What he minded was the fact that she died *forever*.

He would not have stolen from her, but to this new one, this substitute, he owed no allegiance.

If he died, Solo would understand.

When he returned home that evening he found Auntie whispering with Perkins. They were walking about in front of the house pointing to various trees and nodding their heads in agreement. As he approached they both turned to look at him with a careful suspicion.

'Well, what you say?'

'Hello, Auntie.'

'And what about Mr Perkins? Where's your manners? You were brought up, not dragged up.'

'Hello, Mr Perkins.'

Perkins gave a little victorious snort of laughter.

'Hello, young fellow.'

He went into the house as quickly as possible without appearing to be running. The two returned to their whisperings.

Once inside he noticed that things had been moved. Auntie had been preparing. The house now had a new silence. Different even from when the old woman died. Now there was the silence of removal. The silence of empty drawers and walls without photographs.

THE CROSSING

And they tricked him to the sea, saying it was for him. And they betrayed him with kisses and the gentle patting of his head. And first they smiled at him, telling him what a big boy he was and then they moved him on with a gesture.

And when he asked: 'Please, I don't want to go.'

Auntie said: 'No, you going.'

And they turned their faces away from him and looked towards the small army of suitcases and trunks which were being put aboard the ship.

And the first smell of the ship was of oil. And the water was rough, even before its sailing. And because it was early morning the rain fell and he wondered if the rain would make the rising of the sea-swell greater.

And the ship's whistle called out a last warning. And the people waved to him from the dock, and Teacher Biddy held her hat on with her hand and he couldn't tell her crying from the rain and somewhere along the moving pier he could see Solo's cap moving as he ran along the dock. And he did not wave but looked with a look which told him: you will never come back. And he answered him back with a look: unless I dead, Solo.

He felt Auntie's hand. It was not like his mother's. It was hard and strong where hers had been soft and frightened.

The ship moved beneath him or the sea moved. He could not tell which. First they hug you, then they push you away. Into the dark sea waving. And this was manness and alone.

Redemption Song
and other plays

Edgar White

REDEMPTION SONG, THE BOOT DANCE, LES FEMMES NOIRES

These plays by West Indian playwright Edgar White explore the themes of exile, submission and defiance as reflected in black experience.

REDEMPTION SONG is a powerful blend of melodrama and ritual. A poet, Legion Bramble, returns to his island homeland during the Mummers' Festival after an unhappy stay in Britain, to reclaim his West Indian identity.

THE BOOT DANCE, set in an English mental hospital, traces the relationships between Lazarus Mphele, an exiled South African dancer, a cynical West Indian guard named Gibbs, and Janette, a mixed-race teenager who once tried to murder her violent father.

LES FEMMES NOIRES probes the lives of black women in New York A presence in the play - almost a character in its own right - is the omnipresent TV screen, purveyor of cultural values and commodities, which both beckons and excludes those in its sway.

Edgar White was born in Montserrat, West Indies. Five of his plays have been produced by Joseph Papp's New York Shakespeare Theatre. REDEMPTION SONG was premiered at Riverside Studios, London, and THE BOOT DANCE at the Tricycle Theatre, London. His plays are being performed world-wide.